Janice Brown has published five teenage novels and many

GI   10/17   FH 2/2/16

0 1 JUN 2016

2 4 AUG 2016

Gi - Re -auoe
                10/17

Through Every Human Heart

Janice Brown

SANDSTONEPRESS
HIGHLAND | SCOTLAND

First published in Great Britain and the
United States of America 2015
Sandstone Press Ltd
PO Box 5725
One High Street
Dingwall
Ross-shire
IV15 9WJ
Scotland.

www.sandstonepress.com

The publisher acknowledges subsidy from
Creative Scotland towards publication of this volume.

ISBN: 978-1-910124-49-9
ISBN e: 978-1-910124-50-5

Cover design by Rose Cooper, Valencia, Spain
Typeset by Iolaire Typesetting, Newtonmore.
Printed and bound by CPI Group (UK) Ltd, Croydon, CR0 4YY

To Iain and Ruth Laing with love

Acknowledgements

My thanks to Graeme Cuthbertson and Ewen Maclean for all their help.

'Gradually it was disclosed to me that the line separating good and evil passes not through states, nor between classes, nor between political parties either – but right through every human heart – and through all human hearts. This line shifts. Inside us, it oscillates with the years. And even within hearts overwhelmed by evil, one small bridgehead of good is retained.'

Alexander Solzhenitzyn, *The Gulag Archipelago*

Prologue

As they drove on through the gathering dusk, Feliks could still taste the bananas, still smell them on his fingers. He wanted to share the wonder of bananas with the woman beside him but it was impossible. Dina was concentrating on the road, cornering most carefully, never exceeding the speed limit, her hands always in the right position, as if trying to prove herself the perfect driver, to show herself in perfect control of this one thing when the rest of her world was in chaos. She hadn't spoken a word for a long time now, apart from monosyllables in the store at the petrol station.

Even if she got over her anger and began speaking to him again, she wouldn't understand his enthusiasm. Safely packaged in their own smooth skins, highly nutritious, protected from dirt and germs, simple to open, simple to eat, bananas seemed to him to be the embodiment of honesty, almost miraculous in their simplicity and flair. He'd had them at home as a child. Specially imported at Christmas, they were green, hard and bitter. 'You have to be patient, darling. Just a little longer.' But they were so exotic one couldn't wait, even though one still remembered last year's stomach pain.

He glanced over at her. No, she would take bananas for granted, like everything else in her life. In the West everything was taken for granted. Pure water, warm beds, freedom to say what you believed, and as many bananas as you wanted, flown in or shipped in, whichever it was, from their tropical home. He tried to supply the name of the tropical country, but his brain was too tired.

I could live in such a country. I could bear that. I would sit in my backyard all day from dawn to sunset and live on bananas.

He'd watched her relax in the store at the petrol station, glad of her sandwich, and afterwards, blowing like a child on the too-hot soup in its cardboard cup. Her face seemed to soften for a few moments, and he'd felt again how she seduced one's attention – the unsettling, demanding vulnerability that she herself seemed so unconscious of. Now her lips were set in a grim little line.

Since their first meeting he'd been running around like a headless chicken. He'd seen these often enough back home. Fresh from the axe, comical, tragic, the most absurd of sights in an absurd world. Well, this particular chicken had now done something. He'd tried to be heroic. Quite literally he'd given it his best shot.

I don't want to be a hero. I don't want anyone's worship. I don't want to meet anyone's needs or make their dreams come true.

So what do you want, Feliks?

A small house with a banana tree in the garden. Is that too much? One small house, one tree, out of the entire world?

You want your own tree? What would you do, piss on it like a dog? Because that's what you are, Feliks, a dog. A lame, headless chicken of a dog, in need of a tree to piss on.

Chapter One

'What's the matter?' Janek asked.

'It's cold in here,' Lazslo told his boss. It was true, but it was a different sort of cold altogether that was chilling his soul. Memories from his childhood had ambushed him the moment they'd stepped out of the sunlight into this small mountain church, into the sweet-sick smells of tallow and incense, and dust under old pine benches. Twenty years flew from him, like startled sparrows from a bush. He was a child again, in short trousers and a shirt too tight around the neck, staring at a coffin which held what had been his grandfather, the first corpse he'd ever seen. He felt again the rising panic, the desperate desire to escape out into the June sunshine where some of his classmates were joyously, noisily kicking a ball against the poplar trees around the square. When he'd tried to pull free, Grandmother's fingers had tightened on his.

Janek shrugged. 'You're right. We won't linger, I was simply curious.' He turned back to the frescoes.

Was this what they'd come to see? Clothed in sombre red and blue, with no gold to speak of and hardly any silver, all of the saints wore the same strained expression, as if they knew exactly how bad they'd looked when new, and how little faith they would inspire now that so many centuries had come and gone. In other regions, tourists came to visit and admire frescoes. There was no shortage of them. Only a few monasteries still functioned as such of course. Most were museums, though he'd heard of one being turned into a hotel with a gourmet restaurant. This place was too unimportant to matter to anyone.

Certainly Janek had made no attempt to find any human representative of the monastic community, though there were signs of life. A single candle burned at the front of the church. The white cloth on the altar looked clean. A brown clay vase held wild flowers: yellow pulsatilla and white marguerites. He looked up at the ceiling. Plain plasterwork, no coffered wood or intricate designs.

So why were they here? For six hours with only one short break, he had driven from the capital through lush fields of barley, into forests of black, white and grey poplars, then aspen, loud with birdsong, and finally among pines trees on increasingly tortuous, and often shade-free mountain roads. Janek had slept for the latter part of the journey, or pretended to, waking in a strange mood as they neared their destination. He'd become oddly animated, talking rather a lot without saying anything of significance. He was city born and bred, and kept asking statistical questions about the countryside, most of which Lazslo couldn't answer.

The older man turned round. 'Now, my dear, aren't you going to ask me why we've come to Tavcaryeva?'

'Why have we come?'

'To dig up a corpse. There, I knew that would take your fancy. Confess yourself intrigued.'

'I'm intrigued.'

'Of course you are. Even in our line, we don't dig up corpses every day. Now, what do you suggest we do with this corpse once we've brushed off the worms and fat white spiders? Come to that, what shall we do with the worms?'

When his boss was in a mood like this, no answer was

right. He had long ago learned to look diffidently into the air. Sometimes Janek let it pass, and sometimes he didn't.

'Oh don't agitate yourself, our corpse is alive. Shall we?'

Outside, it had somehow become late afternoon. Their path went along a brief avenue of not very tall white poplars, then under a low stone archway into a walled kitchen garden, larger than he expected. It was south facing, criss-crossed by elderly and very gnarled fruit trees, plum and apple he recognised, their fruit still forming. Between them two Angry Birds darted suddenly, one after the other, in well-practised zigzags, from one side of the orchard up into the same tree, their gold heads and black wing feathers etched clear against the pale peach breasts. The light itself here seemed golden, almost dreamlike, though after a moment he detected a faint smell of something like creosote on the air. There was a large compost heap against the far wall, and four long raised beds. He guessed the planks had been recently re-coated. He couldn't quite make out what was growing in the reddish soil. Potatoes, beets, onions, he supposed, though this high up, everything would need a fair bit of manure. The winter would be cold. He could hear the squawking and clucking of hens somewhere beyond the high wall. Chicken for supper, perhaps. Not so very bad.

'There he is,' Janek said.

The priest was young, about his own age, bearded, strongly built. He was in clerical garb, but had stripped to the waist, working with a spade in a row of small but healthy-looking purple cabbages.

As they came closer, the man straightened.

'How are you, Feliks?' Janek said.

Lazslo looked more closely and felt something inside him rip apart.

No one spoke. A loose cloud of Large Copper butterflies

flew gaudily round about them then flew on. The leaves on the fruit trees were completely motionless, as if they were too preoccupied with sunlight to do anything but breathe.

Finally Janek said, 'The monastic life must agree with you, Feliks. I see you've developed a fine pair of biceps, whatever else you've been up to.'

'And what have you been up to? Still licking my father's ass?'

The spade sliced into the ground with a blow that would have severed a spine. Janek made a slight tutting sound.

'Come now, don't be like that. We've come an exceedingly long way. I thought you'd be glad to see some visitors from outside. And I was sure you two would be overjoyed at seeing one another again. Father Konstantin has given us the use of his room,' he added. 'We'll wait for you there, Feliks. Don't be too long. Lazslo?'

Barely able to see his surroundings, Laszlo followed. Every moment of the way he listened and hoped and kept hoping. But there were no footsteps behind him, no movement, no calling of his name.

Chapter Two

In the wash-house Feliks pumped fresh water into the bowl, then splashed it over his head and arms and upper body. He stood upright, took the piece of canvas from its hook and began to rub himself dry. Then with a curse he flung it away, and smashed his fists against the sink. For a moment or two he stood there, before sliding down onto his knees. Janek's face took shape in the throbbing darkness, and behind it, Lazslo's, white as a bare root.

Lazslo of all people. What had Janek told him to get him here? What threats? What promises? For all his irritating ways, there had always been something endearing about him. They'd nicknamed him Squirrel because of his reddish hair and his amazing ability to remember things, like a squirrel hiding its nuts away, although someone pointed out that squirrels forgot many times where they'd hidden food, and Lazslo forgot nothing, so it wasn't altogether apt. The nickname stuck because he was such a fearful soul, so nervous, always darting glances sideways, waiting for the sky to fall on them.

Why had Janek brought him? Why had they come?

He had not foreseen this. He wasn't ready. The walls that surrounded him seemed to melt, becoming what scientists said they had always been, not solid, but merely atoms moving at great speed.

His hands were shaking. Really shaking. He almost laughed. Once upon a time he'd been ready for anything.

Perfectly in control, with no self-doubt, no regrets, and none of the pointless introspection he'd seen and despised in those around him.

More than three years ago when he'd arrived at Tavcarjeva, he'd been close to death, a wreck, physically and mentally, or so they told him. (Was it late winter or early spring? The brothers would know; he wasn't certain.) They had nursed him back to life. 'Death is not an accident,' they said. 'It is God's doing.' What they wouldn't say was how he'd reached them, or who had borne him to their isolated mountain top, to sensory deprivation, silence, darkness and vacancy, an emptiness that gradually eased its way into one's bones. Plain food and plain chant became his existence. When eventually he could move about, they'd suggested the garden. It had been turning increasingly to wilderness before his coming. He'd been sent by God, they told him. This he doubted, but let them believe what they wanted to. They were so old and fragile, so well-meaning, solemn and undemanding, and he didn't have the energy to argue. Then by the time he could think straight, he found they had crept into his bones along with the silence. He couldn't bear to disappoint them or undermine their certainties.

He'd begun to work in the garden, weeding, pruning, sweeping leaves, then onto the harder work. Seeds and plants had arrived, some had taken, some hadn't. The fruit trees, especially the plums, had astonished everyone. There had even been an attempt at jam.

But while the days had become bearable, the nights had become harder for quite some time. Memories returned. In the dark his former companions came to him, with bemused, bewildered faces. Anna came to him. *Go away*, he told her. *You shouldn't be here, you're dead. You know you're dead.* And though in his dreams he invoked

8

the names of the Father, Son and Holy Ghost, and all the Saints he could think of, they did nothing to help. If such beings existed, they were all on her side. They knew why she was dead. They knew whose fault it was.

The months had passed and when word of the regime's fall reached the tiny village and its monastery, it seemed to meander in most casually, as unremarkable as the smell of supper's barley soup. Ageing, yet somehow untroubled by age, the brothers seemed to breathe a communal sigh. *God's doing.* Governments and ideologies were passing vanities. Eternal truths, prayer and silence were all that mattered, and ultimately, only silence. Tavcarjeva, isolated, unimportant, faint pinprick on a faded map, held all safe. He had been lulled into its careless waking slumber.

Time to wake up, Feliks Berisovic. Whether you are ready or not.

Chapter Three

The Abbot's room refused to belong to any century in particular. Neither mediaeval nor modern, it appeared to Lazslo to succeed in what seemed an earnest attempt to imitate the sanctuary itself in drabness and mediocrity. The open window looked out onto a grassy expanse, with troughs of nettles and herbs, then to the wooden fence and the narrow approach road. He caught mint, lavender and something that might have been fennel, but most likely wasn't, not at this altitude. There was one cushioned armchair near the fireplace. It might be worth something, if it wasn't a reproduction. He could tell Janek was thinking the same thing. The material was tapestry, picturing the grape harvest, little mediaeval men and women in groups accepting tankards and carrying baskets of fruit to the cart. Very traditional, often copied. A little odd for it to be here.

Janek seated himself after inspecting the room. He made a face, obviously finding the armchair less comfortable than he had expected. There was a bare stone fireplace, and beside it an unsafe-looking electric fire, encased in steel. An oak bookcase, without glass, held a dozen or so hardback books with illegible titles on the spines. A matching table and four upright high-backed chairs, a couple of paintings on wood, and a floor lamp with a white fringed shade on a metal stand were all the other furniture. In contrast to all this serious poverty, an ornate silver coffee pot and matching cups had been set out for them on a silver tray. The coffee proved to be excellent.

The minutes limped by. Lazslo held his cup in both hands, trying to relax, knowing that Janek was only pretending not to watch him. He felt he had never hated the man more. As for Feliks . . . No, he refused to go there . . .

He drained the cup, replaced it on the tray, sat down and picked up a small ivory, or perhaps bone, Pieta from the bookcase beside him. The knife strokes were unsubtle. There was no maker's name underneath.

He resisted the urge to check his watch.

What if Feliks didn't come, and he, Lazslo, was sent from the room to find him? What if he couldn't be found?

'Macabre, don't you think?' Janek said suddenly, pointing to a triptych above the fireplace.

They might take the car, it was possible, he had the keys in his pocket. Feliks might say, 'Drive to the border,' and they might drive to the border, stop just before it where the forest offered plenty of cover . . .

'Whose head would it be, I wonder?'

'It's possibly John the Baptist.'

'What a mine of eclectic information you are, my dear. Tell me, what did he do? Why is he on a plate?'

'Herod killed his brother and married the widow. The Baptist reprimanded him in public, so Herod had him killed.'

'Herod?'

'The king at the time. Of Jerusalem. Around 29AD.'

Janek stroked the arm of the chair, pushing the cloth back and forth. His fingernails were so smooth Lazslo suspected he polished them. Certainly he coloured his receding hair, or had it coloured for him. There was grey at the temples but nowhere else. Knowing this was the most miniscule of comforts, but Lazslo had clung to it many, many times.

11

'Dear me,' Janek said. 'A lesson to us all.'

'A lesson?'

'Here we are, Lazslo, earnest servants of the new democracy, yet we must remain vigilant. We must not displease our superiors, or even our heads may roll. So tell me,' he poured himself more coffee, 'what did you think of our corpse? For myself, I don't think I would have known him, if we'd passed in the street. Not that one would ever have classed him as handsome. One wonders what his fond Papa will say.' He crossed one leg over the other, and brushed his trouser cuff as if as if some irritating red dust from the garden had clung to him. 'I must say I had hoped for a little more enthusiasm, Lazslo. You and Feliks were quite intimate once, they tell me.'

Loosen the leash then jerk it a little. It was Janek's favourite game. Lazslo pictured a chain below the older man's chin, watched a line of dark blood form then begin to ooze, trickling down the white collar onto the shirt . . .

'Well, weren't you?'

'We weren't in the same year.'

'You published that bold, seditious rag together. You were close.'

'No. He wasn't . . . We weren't friends.'

It was a lie. Or was it true? Had he really been any different from the others, anything more than a blind worshipper? The whole thing had been furiously intoxicating because Feliks was who he was, the rebel son of the most hated man in the regime. Feliks was dangerous, bold, invincible. But friendship would have been as impossible as kissing incandescence.

Janek drained his cup. 'It doesn't surprise me. Men like him rarely make many friends. They're too full of their own self-righteousness to be bothered with the likes of you and me. We bore them.'

'Maybe he won't come.'

'Oh, he'll come. He's making us wait, but he'll come. He has no choice. You know, this is remarkable coffee. I wonder where they get it from. They might make their own brandy too. Places like this often have a little secret cellar worth looking into. So you weren't close, even when you worked side by side?'

'It was a committee. And as you say, he was a loner. We hardly saw him.'

Janek stretched and smiled. 'This will amuse you, Lazslo. Do you know, the thought had actually entered my mind that you might have known he was here all the time?'

'I thought he was dead. Everyone did.'

This was true. Despite his fears, he had gone with everyone to the graveyard, devastated, frozen half to death themselves in the whirling snow. A week later he'd been summoned to the police station. Two days after that he had found himself working for Janek.

'My dear, you're going to break her if you continue to rub so fiercely.'

Lazslo looked down. The Madonna was still in his hands. He put her back on the shelf.

Janek continued, 'I'm so relieved you weren't keeping things from me. I should have believed Vasreche after all.'

'Vasreche?'

'The name rings no bells? Ah well, he professed not to recognise yours either. Sometimes it's so hard to know. He sweated terribly, I remember. He became quite incoherent towards the end.'

He couldn't recall the name. As Janek's secretary, he had access to everything but he couldn't recall the name. So there was no file.

'You can't imagine the trouble I had convincing Vasreche that his information about Feliks wasn't going to get him off the hook. He'd been here and hereabouts in the autumn looking for something, manuscripts of some sort, relics, it hardly matters. He'd seen our friend, recognised him despite the . . . how shall we put it?, Alterations . . . and talked about it to some of his cronies.'

'And he came to you.'

'Well, not willingly. Very few people come to me willingly.'

Was this directed at him? Probably. It didn't matter. What mattered was the shock he'd seen in Feliks' eyes. What mattered was what Feliks was presently thinking, what Feliks was going to say to him. He wondered at his continued ability to speak coherently, to hear what Janek was saying.

'He'd held some temporary post in the History Department at the University before he entered his life of crime. I thought you might have known him.'

'But I was in Computing Science. And I was two years behind Berisovic. It must have been before I got there.'

'Quite right. Vasreche was dismissed the term before you began. And besides, you would have had nothing in common. He was a man with no principles, no respect for authority. So you really didn't know Berisovic was here.'

'He was dead. His father was at the funeral, you yourself . . .'

'I know, I know. Tell me, what do you think we should do with him, now that he's alive?'

His mind faltered, his tongue lay in his mouth dry as a dead leaf.

At last Janek leaned back in his chair. 'Why do I ask you? Forgive me, my dear, I'm a sentimental fool. It's neither your decision nor mine.'

Chapter Four

Smart casual, Irene had told them. No long dresses, no formal suits. Several of the men were in kilts though. Dina liked to see men in kilts, as long as they had decent calf muscles. Not every man could wear a kilt. Members of rugby teams wore them admirably as a rule. There wasn't much to beat a rugby player in a kilt.

She'd tried to time her arrival early enough to avoid Irene's disapproval, but not so early as to be among the first present. There wasn't a bar, just tables with chairs round them, name-cards on the tables and little plates of peanuts and snacks. She'd learned from bitter experience that it was a serious mistake to sit anywhere at the beginning, or indeed the middle, of any social function, for so many different reasons, so she stayed on her feet.

'Three line whip tonight,' Irene had reminded everyone. It was a charity auction for endangered animals, hosted by a well-known Bank whose new offices they had furnished, with a few other important client firms invited. Dina felt mildly hypocritical, knowing she wasn't nearly as concerned about saving the planet as she ought to be.

White voile curtains hid the evening sky. Mindless music flowed. Massive pompoms made of tissue paper hung from the low ceiling: black and white striped, in imitation, she guessed, of zebras, and brown spots on beige, which might have been anything really, giraffes or leopards, or even pigs, except that pigs weren't endangered. The tables were close to the podium, but most of the guests were still standing in groups behind them. Immense photos of the creatures which would benefit from the evening were arranged round the walls: snow leopards, tigers and pandas, insects and birds, reptiles she'd never seen or heard of. Women in the Bank's trademark colours were standing around with programmes and information packs. They were uniformly slim and good-looking. Were they actual Bank staff?

Expect some famous faces, Irene had said. Probably they were too famous to come on time. The cheery leader of the city council was cheerily holding court, and she recognised one woman who did the news on STV, and a middle-aged comedian she'd never much liked, and someone who she thought might be a famous footballer, but no one from Arbanisi Design, except the middle-aged man with the tinted glasses who did something somewhere on their top floor. He was standing by himself, poor soul.

Then she saw Paul, looking very grand, contemplating a bronze abstract wall sculpture. He turned, noticed her and raised a friendly eyebrow. She manoeuvred her way to him through drifts of aftershave and perfume. She recognised Anais Anais. That was an old one. Mother had worn it a lot.

Paul was committed to his lover too firmly to allow one any hope, but being around him always made Dina feel better. He gave her a sense that life could be managed. Not completely of course – she wasn't that stupid, life would always be a bit confusing sometimes – but when you were with Paul, you felt that there were answers around if you just thought about things more carefully. Irene, naturally blond, mid-thirties, currently single, was the founder and ideas person in Arbanisi Design. Paul, a little older, with wavy black hair greying so beautifully, dealt with difficulties and made the ideas happen. Arbanisi Design was small compared with many other companies, but it was Irene's baby and she didn't want it to grow much bigger, and neither did Paul.

'Hello, my best girl,' he said. She'd been charmed by this greeting in her first weeks with the firm, until she realized that he said it to all the women in Arbanisi Design, even the two harridans in the showroom. Actually she was still charmed. It had become something of a continuing challenge to make sure she was the 'best' best girl.

He seemed to be without his partner.

'A three piece suit? Isn't that breaking the rules?' Dina said, lightly prodding his waistcoat.

'Shoot me,' he said.

'Will I do?' she asked.

'Oh, very nicely' Paul smiled.

She was learning. To conceal her non-ideal waist, she was wearing a loose silk top. Loose but not completely liberated. No bra straps peeping out, and strictly no cleavage. Her breasts were too much without encouragement. Cropped trousers to make her look taller and show off her neat ankles. The shoes were daring but not wildly so. She could walk quite far in them, if need be.

'Of course, the success of your evening may also depend on the state of your bank balance.'

He meant the auction.

'Not good this month,' she said.

'Then no reckless bidding, please, especially for Irene's things.'

'I promise to be good. What did she decide on?'

'The cigarette case.' He flipped open the schedule. ' "A beautiful piece of Imperial Russian art",' he read. ' "Solid silver, gilded inside and out, polychrome cloisonné enamel in seven colours." '

'Do people still buy cigarette cases?'

'I'm sure some do. But she's put the peacock thing in as well. It'll probably reach four figures. Rescuing these poor lemurs and sand cats is very close to our Wise Leader's heart.'

'I liked that pendant.'

'But you wouldn't wear it, sweetheart,' he said. 'Too fantastic, too big, and way too many sapphires for you. To wear that very expensive chunk of old Central European bling you would need to be . . .'

She interrupted, not much wanting to be told what she would need to be. 'That looks completely right, doesn't it?' she went on, pointing to the bronze statuary. Paul had been a bit wary about it mid-contract.

'Oh definitely,' Paul nodded. 'Context is all.' He lifted his glass to a passing couple, 'No escort tonight?'

'Gone to London to sort something.'

'Silly fool.' He put his free arm round her shoulder and gave her a brief squeeze. 'Let's get you a drink.'

This done, he excused himself, and wandered away to chat to someone else, confident, she imagined, that she was a big grown up girl who would swim and not sink. If Derek had been able to come, she thought, this would have been less stressful. Or just a different stress?

Derek ticked most of the boxes. She enjoyed the way he looked at her, but she was beginning to feel mildly claustrophobic. He was sometimes a teeny wee bit too complimentary. 'You look lovely' would have done, instead of going into detail, and asking where she'd bought this or that. She didn't want to lie, but sometimes it wasn't much fun to have to admit that your striking new top had come from Tesco rather than Next, with mother-of-pearl buttons substituted by yourself for the unstriking originals. And for someone in such an important job, with so many people underneath him, Derek's mind seemed to work in an awfully ordinary way. Or was she being unfair? Her own mind wasn't that interesting. She hadn't got nearly good enough results at school to get into Medicine, and had just scraped into the nursing degree course. But four months into their relationship, she felt there should still be surprises. Or maybe a few profound thoughts. Like: were they meant for each other, and was she the most wonderful woman he'd ever met?

'Does he make you laugh, honey?' was Ronni's question.

'Of course,' she said, for they did laugh a lot. But when she'd thought about it later, she wondered if they just laughed together at things. Which of course was a good sign. Just not exactly what Ronni had meant.

She had perfected his mother's lasagne recipe to please his Italian taste buds, but his soul seemed to be solidly Glaswegian, like his father's. And he was awfully, well . . . clean. Not a problem in itself, of course. Nobody in their right mind wanted to wake up next to smelly armpits. She just wondered if he was more interested in deodorants than destiny. 'Release others to their destiny and claim yours.' She'd read that once in Marie Claire. She liked the idea of having a destiny. On the other hand, Derek had a lot going for him. It was difficult. Maybe she needed to rethink the boxes.

She caught sight of Irene, encircled mostly by men, her blond hair loose around her tanned shoulders. Dina's heart slipped a little. She loved dresses like the one Irene was wearing, but her own waist was basically in the wrong place. She'd worked that one out for herself at thirteen, when her growth stopped, after studying a picture of the dancer Margot Fonteyn, who'd been perfectly proportioned. In summer she felt more hard-done-to than in winter, because there were so many gorgeous simple dresses, so easy to accessorize. She loved big hats, but they made

19

her look like a mushroom, wide on top above a dumpy stem. She never wore flat shoes because they made her look short. Only the week before, a bin lorry had almost reversed into her. 'Watch that wee wumman,' someone had shouted. She'd told the story against herself at work. A 'wumman' at twenty-six. And 'wee'.

Paul came back, introducing her to a man with a tartan bow tie and spiky dark hair rising from a big forehead. She missed the name, but caught the fact that he worked for the Bank.

'We're really pleased with all you did,' he said.

'I'm glad to hear it. It was a fascinating . . .'

'And I gather you work directly with the boss lady?' He looked towards Irene. 'Not an easy person to work with, I imagine. Doesn't she scare you?'

'No,' she said, puzzled by the question. What did he mean? It was a great job. They had a great time together. Irene knew what she wanted in a personal assistant and Dina did what was needed. Irene liked making choices. She liked not having to make choices.

'You must be braver than you look,' he said with a laugh, showing all his teeth. His upper ones were fine, but the lower ones were kind of crushed together.

'So what do you do in your time off?' he asked.

'I like to cook,' she said, 'especially for men who like to eat.'

'That sounds interesting.'

It always did, which was why she said it every time. It wasn't hard to sound interesting. Or look interesting, if you had DD breasts and the man you were with cared about that sort of thing. Herself, she wished she could have a smaller bust and a bigger brain, and actually be more interesting than she looked. And more real and far more honest. And braver. Another one to add to the list apparently. His lower teeth looked miserably unhappy. Dare she mention orthodontics? She'd worn braces, top and bottom, for two years, but the pain had been worth it. Was that brave?

He chatted on above the music, she nodded and smiled. Was she brave? She had nothing to be brave about. Coming south to Glasgow hadn't been brave. What was there to be afraid of in life, apart from the usual things, like gaining weight, or deleting something important or seeing a daddy-long-legs in the bedroom just as the light went out?

Now he was talking about his last holiday in the Swiss Alps. She mentioned her childhood home and its mountains. He was interested but not so much. Switzerland was so clean, and so reliable, everything there was done properly . . .

You could be afraid of never finding true love, she thought. If you wanted to. If you wanted to let your mind dwell on such a thing when you woke too early and couldn't get back to sleep. She wanted to ask Mr Tartan Tie if he believed in Destiny, but it seemed unkind to distract him from his exploits off piste. She'd learned long ago the trick of listening without hearing. When she was still a teenager she'd deliberately let one of her father's GP trainees talk and talk to her at the dinner table for fourteen minutes.

She smiled and nodded as Mr Tartan and his broken leg were airlifted from the slopes above Wengen and taken to Interlaken.

Of course, if you were thinking very deeply and foolishly, and didn't have all that many friends because you were rubbish at keeping in touch, you could fear the prospect of dying dehydrated and alone in a hospital bed. It happened every day.

'Actually I trained as a nurse originally,' she told him.

He took this as permission to describe the fracture and surgery in detail, including the costs.

Whatever her destiny was, it hadn't been nursing. That had just brought out the worst in her. Being a PA was more satisfying. She was learning so much. Irene was teaching her about aesthetics, what worked and what didn't and why, and the exposure to colour and creativity made her feel much happier about life.

Just as she was wondering how to detach herself, she caught sight of Irene, gesturing her towards their table. The music faded and a man with a deep bass voice was announcing on the microphone that the main business of the evening was about to begin, and please give a warm welcome to your host for the evening, who was the comedian she didn't like. There was an enthusiastic round of applause.

Mr Tartan Tie reached into his pocket for a card. 'In case you ever want to speculate.'

'Speculate?'

'Investment advice.'

'Oh right. If I ever come into some money.' She smiled back. As if she would. As if that was what he meant.

She gave him a nice but non-committal wave and seated herself at her place, studying the programme. When she looked up, the Great Indian Bustard on the wall seemed to be looking down its long beak at her with a dour and disapproving eye.

Chapter Five

Feliks closed the door behind him. He looked first at Lazslo but he seemed fascinated by the stone floor, and didn't look up. There was a rich smell of coffee in the air. Not for him perhaps. Janek was playing with the lid of the silver coffee pot, tracing its fine Byzantine lines. There were only two cups on the tray. Definitely not for him then.

Was *he* meant to speak first? He would not. He was used to silence now, and willing to bet he could endure it longer than Janek. And he was right.

'Do sit down, Feliks. You make me nervous, hovering like that.'

He'd been in this room before, but didn't remember it well. He turned one of the chairs round, hitching his cassock above his trousers, so that he could sit astride, facing Janek over its back, as if he were the questioner, not the accused. Carefully he folded his arms, in case his hands betrayed him again.

Janek got the symbolism at once, and stood up, stretching as if his back was stiff. He began moving around the room.

'Such a long drive we've had to get here, so far from all the dust and grime. This high mountain air must be very beneficial, Feliks. For someone who's been dead for almost four years, you look astonishingly robust.'

Dead? So that was why he'd been left alone. How had it been done? He glanced at Lazslo, willing him to look round.

23

'You didn't know? How fascinating. You died and were buried, my dear. There was a decent crowd, suitably distressed, and snow falling in graceful sympathy on your coffin from a leaden sky. The Boss didn't cry, but I could tell he was moved. There were no photographs, but you had an inch or two in the newspaper. If they could see you now, I believe they'd be rather taken by your manly vitality. You must pause before every mirror you pass.'

'They don't have mirrors here. God looks into the soul and sees the truth.'

'Is that so? What a quaint idea. And such a troublesome concept. *The truth is always an abyss.* Kafka, I believe. But you were always such an energetic thinker, such a ruthless pursuer of ideas.'

'Whereas you were merely ruthless.'

When had Janek started reading Kafka? It wasn't at all likely. The man hadn't the brain power.

'Dear me, we are a little tetchy today. I thought this life was meant to induce serenity. Very different from your dashing past activities. It struck me as we stepped through the gate, that all this was exactly not you. You were always so keen on taking charge of things and now here you are in a tight little world of self-denial, where a hen is the closest you can get to a vagina. . . .'

'Cut the shit. Why are you here?'

'Your father sent me.'

It came like a slap in the face. But it was possible. Janek had never had an original thought in his life. He was at the bookcase now, pulling out the fragile books, pretending to read the title pages.

'You've never actually taken vows, I'm told. What stopped you? You could have risen to some kind of eminence here, surely. I can't *quite* imagine you as our national copy of Rasputin, the beard isn't nearly long enough for one thing.' Finding his fingers dusty, he wiped them against one another, with an expression of distaste. 'Enough of my prattling. As I said, your father wants to see you.'

'I don't believe you.'

'But he does. I assure you, his very words. 'Tell the laddie I need to see him.'

'So where is he? In jail or on his death bed?'

'What strange ideas you have, Feliks. Your father is where he always was. In charge. Oh, don't glower at me like that. It's perfectly true. The wording on the door is different, of course. We keep in step with the times.'

Feliks looked from Janek to Lazslo, seeking confirmation. Or something. Anything. But Lazslo was still staring at the floor.

'Why does he want to see me?'

For the first time he sensed a hesitation. Janek seemed to be pausing to think, choosing his words instead of merely blabbing on.

'I don't know.'

It sounded like the truth.

'That must hurt,' Feliks said. 'After all these years.'

'But you know how secretive he likes to be. On the other hand, I *was* the only one he trusted enough to come and get you. Nobody else knows you're alive. I take no end of comfort from that.'

In the past Janek wouldn't have dared operate independently, so presumably he *was* here on Boris's instructions. Of course those instructions might say that he was to be taken from the monastery to be killed somewhere on the road. Most likely Lazslo had been brought along to confirm the identification, and then to be killed as well. There was an air of profound misery surrounding him, as if that very expectation was in his mind.

'Supposing I don't want to come.'

Janek frowned. 'Do you know, I don't think that possibility occurred to him? One of the drawbacks of getting your own way all the time. Now, *I'm* different. I so rarely get my own way. Constantly I worry that things might turn out badly. Life can be so fragile. That very word occurred to me when Father Konstantin was speaking to us earlier. I think it was something about the slenderness of his aged neck. Did I speak to you about it, Lazslo?'

Lazslo jumped.

'I . . . I don't remember.'

'You don't remember? How unlike you. Your memory is one of your finest qualities. Do you know, Feliks, since Lazslo began working for me, not long after your death in fact, I hardly write anything down. He's quite amazing. A real treasure.'

Working for him? No, it wasn't possible . . .

'. . . don't know how I'd have got through these troublesome years without him at my side. He's a mine of information, a veritable mine. Come to think of it, I expect he remembers every miserable detail of your funeral, including his own tears. I'll get him to write it all down for you.'

The room grew cold. Smaller. Feliks felt suddenly aware of his own breathing. The quickest of glances told him that Lazslo was now looking at him. He closed his eyes.

'I do believe we've tired you, my dear. I'm tired myself. Why don't you take a little time to think things through? We're going to stay overnight. Those roads are ghastly in daylight; they would be more or less suicidal in the dark. And we can't have that again, can we?'

Chapter Six

Even though the car windows were closed, Feliks could taste the dust as they drove down through the narrow pass. Here and there, a thin aspen had seeded in a crack in the red rock walls and a few spindly bellflowers clung to the barren outcrops. Soon there were more trees, and more houses. They passed a river where a wooden watermill slowly rotated its wheel in the unrushed current.

He tried to distract himself with Kafka. (He was sure Janek had merely picked up his quote second-hand, scavenged it from somewhere, like a rat on the municipal dump, not even understanding its meaning.) A Jew, a vegetarian, and a sufferer of TB. Dead at forty. So if he were Kafka, almost three quarters of his life would be gone. He didn't know much about the man, having only read a couple of books in translation. He'd found them strange and clever, if unsatisfying, though not as old-fashioned as he'd expected for someone who'd lived so long ago. Of course the translations were modern.

But nothing could long distract him from the turmoil of his own thoughts. *What can I do? Why does he want me?* The questions repeated themselves. He still wore his cassock. There was apparently nothing else to change into. His old clothes had been bloodstained beyond repair, burned long ago. He had slept fitfully, trying to imagine some alternative to leaving with Janek, but none presented itself. He didn't want the brothers to be harmed. It was one thing to be irritated by watery eyes and dripping noses, quite another to give Janek an excuse to drop frail old bones under his heel. He had always hated his father's number one, and hated him still. It was easy to listen to sermons about loving one's enemy. Impossible in practice. Janek was now in the front passenger seat, snoring, his forehead glistening, a bottle of plum brandy at his feet, and he imagined, several more in the car boot.

Lazslo was driving. He wanted to hate Lazslo too, but it was hard. When he looked at Lazslo, he felt so much anger and frustration it was exhausting. Pity? No, he wouldn't admit to feeling sorry for him. Everyone made their own choices. There was a small bald patch on the back of Lazlso's head beneath the red brown curls. Was he aware of it? If he was, perhaps he didn't care. Vanity had never been one of his faults. Vanity would have been better than this. Vanity would have been understandable. He had never had much success with women despite his good looks. A lack of confidence had made him his own worst enemy in that department. But it would be wrong to feel pity for him now. You make your bed, you lie in it. *Cut him adrift, forget him*, his mind advised.

As they dropped further down into the valley, the volume of traffic increased, though they were still a long way from real civilization. Everything conspired to slow their progress. Lazslo used the horn from time to time to very little effect. He steered the big car carefully round broken-down buses, people who'd stopped to buy watermelons at the roadside, white geese waddling in the stirring dust with equally lazy children watching over them, carts laden and lopsided with summer vegetables. Feliks thought longingly about watermelon, imagining luscious scarlet slices of it filling his mouth. The brothers had provided goat cheese and rye bread, nothing wrong with that, but only small bottles of water, not enough for the three of them.

Now and again he noticed wreaths of dried flowers on fences and roadside trees, something he'd never seen before. Memorials to accidents he supposed. A new tradition, imported from where? Would he find other things changed?

If he'd been warned of their coming, what would he have done? Stupor in the face of clearly approaching disaster was ingrained in him, as in so many of his fellow countrymen, a national characteristic like olive skin and long noses. It was as if they were predestined to live out the tales told in childhood. In every story, evil prospered because the good did nothing. Consider the shepherd whose magic sheep warn him that two rival shepherds are about to kill him for his gold. Instead of fleeing, the rich shepherd goes home to put his affairs in order and waits to be murdered.

They passed through rose fields and the perfume filled the car. He recalled a scarred table, scattered with white petals. Victor's apartment, the autumn of his own first year at the University. Someone produces a mandolin. They sing all the old mournful folk songs, inventing salacious words when no one can remember the correct ones. The talk turns to politics, but someone bangs on the table, making the petals flutter, and says, none of that tonight. They all laugh and agree, because they know they are going to change the world, so what does one night off matter?

He'd been the newcomer, the youngest there that night, and because he wanted to observe everything and everyone, he'd remained resolutely sober. He walked a girl home in light September rain. She'd asked him to because her boyfriend was too drunk. He remembered how tightly she had held on to him because of the slippery lime-tree leaves underfoot. At her apartment door, she kissed him on the

29

mouth. It was a delight, she said, to find someone among Victor's friends who could be trusted not to put a hand up her. Since Boris had introduced him to the delights of women as part of his sixteenth birthday celebrations, the unsought and undeserved compliment made Feliks want to giggle, but he'd managed not to. It was a long walk back to his house, with his mind on fire. He'd lain down on the bed with the feel of her lips still on his, kneading her imagined breasts until relief came.

Chapter Seven

Feliks woke when they stopped in a deeply-shadowed street of old buildings. Fatigue, comfortable seating and the steady, quiet rumble of the engine had conspired against him. He didn't recognise the area. Directly beside them was the ornate pillared frontage of what looked like a public bathhouse. A couple of teenagers were walking along the narrow pavement towards them, with a thin black dog on a lead. It looked like a young dog, but one hind leg was missing. It stopped to pee against one of the pillars. The girl kept her eye on the dog, but the boy looked at the big Dacia and its tinted windows.

'Where are we?' he asked Janek.

'Zdravets.'

'You said we were going to the capital.'

'All in good time, dear boy. Shall we go in? Punctuality gives him such pleasure.'

Lazslo waited in the car.

'Smoke if you must,' Janek told him, 'But leave the window open.'

The heavy outer doors were locked, and a printed notice read, 'Closed for maintenance and repair.' However, when Janek pulled on the bell, a smaller side door opened almost at once. They stepped through into a high-walled, ceramic-tiled passage, open to the evening sky. The attendant, a young dark-haired man, went ahead of them and opened another door into a small room, where

Janek switched on the light and seated himself beside a wooden table, picking up what might have been the day's newspaper.

'On you go,' he said.

'By myself?'

'Oh, he sees me all the time. I'd hate to intrude on such a reunion.'

So his father was here, waiting for him. His mouth was suddenly dry.

'How do you know I won't find another exit, once I'm out of sight?'

'I trust you completely. And you would merely be delaying the inevitable.'

Feliks followed the attendant into a dressing room with peeling, green-painted walls, numbered lockers and a tiled floor which smelled strongly of disinfectant.

'Please, sir.'

The young man was holding out a large white towel. It finally dawned on Feliks that he was meant to strip and wear the towel. His clothes were picked up, folded and slid into a wire mesh basket. In the next room, the heat caught at his chest. It was empty and noiseless, apart from a faint hushing from the pipes. They moved next through a dim corridor and into a warm dry room, circular, perhaps fifteen metres in diameter. The door closed with a hushed thud behind the retreating attendant. Feliks caught the unmistakeable scent of fig oil. There were two men in the room, one standing, the other lying on his stomach. The first was Dimitar, in a black sleeveless t-shirt. The silver haired one, lying on the massage table, was his father. His face was turned away. Feliks willed Dimitar to look up. Just once, he pleaded. *Just once.* But it was a re-enactment of his first encounter with Lazslo. The old man was intent on his work, massaging Boris's back with long, smooth

32

strokes. So, his back was still troubling him. Excellent.

Above them the domed ceiling was dark against the night outside, but the lowest circles of its small coloured bullions of blue and lilac gleamed slightly, reflecting the glow from a series of glass-encased wall lights. There was no other door. The tiled walls curved around him, in an interlocking formulaic pattern of knights on horseback, with stringed bows and long lances, round and round with no crack or imperfection. It was a room fit for silent whispers, old treasons, foul conspiracies.

Boris raised one hand, signalling for the massage to cease. He sat up, glanced over, then reached for a towel and patted his face and neck for several seconds.

'Feliks. Come closer. Take the stool,' he said.

Feliks went closer, but did not sit. His tongue felt as if it was stuck to the roof of his mouth. He could feel his heart beat.

His father smiled. 'What can I say? I feel I should say something memorable. It's not every day a man gets to meet a son who's risen from the dead.'

At last Dimitar looked up. Some kind of emotion crossed his face. Feliks couldn't read it.

'I hope you didn't mind my sending Janek for you. He's a bit of a slob but at least he does what he's told to do without fussing, which is a rare quality these days. So how long has it been, anyway? Three years now?'

'Why am I here?' Feliks said.

'I wanted to see you, naturally. It's not every father who weeps for a dead son, then finds him alive.'

'You wept for me?'

'You're my only son. Of course I wept for you.'

This was so patently a lie that Feliks wanted to laugh.

'God forgive you,' he said.

'Why do you say that?'

'Suicide is a mortal sin. One shouldn't weep for a suicide.'

'So it *was* a suicide attempt.'

'A poor one, but mine own.'

'Why?'

'I must have thought it was a good idea. I was full of good ideas at the time.'

Boris seemed slightly unsettled, as if he didn't know how to respond.

He'd always had back trouble. Now he was rubbing his knees, first one then the other, as if they, unlike Janek, were not behaving as they'd been told to. He'd be past sixty now, Feliks thought. Still impressive, but there was more flesh round the waist, less silver hair at the temples.

'Why don't you lie down?' Boris suggested. 'You must be tired after such a long journey. Let Dimitar give you a massage.'

Feliks unrolled the blue towel on the adjoining table and lay down on his back, so that he could see his father out of the corner of his eye, and more importantly, look up at Dimitar's face. The oil spreading on his chest and shoulders was warm, fig-scented. But Dimitar's upside down face was closed, only his fingers were alive, pressing, probing, deeper into the chest and shoulder muscles . . .

'We'll not talk about the past,' Boris began. 'What you did is your business. Over and done with. What matters now is where we go from here.'

'We?'

'Well, why not? We've both changed, Feliks. You've grown up, and I'm . . . well, I'm growing old, though I'm loath to admit it. I've learned a lot in the last few years. About life, about myself. It's not been easy, believe me. I suppose what it boils down to is that I've had to rethink my whole philosophy.'

34

Dimitar's fingers seemed to pause, to press harder, until they almost hurt.

'I've had an increasing sense of foreboding,' Boris went on, 'a sense that time is running short, if this country of ours is to survive long enough to become an independent true democracy. You never thought you'd hear me talk this way, did you? So, what do you say? Will you help me?'

'How could I help you?' As he spoke, he felt the pressure of Dimitar's fingers lift and press down hard again. What was his old friend was trying to tell him?

'I need someone I can trust.'

'And you think it's me.'

'Yes.'

Fuck this. He swung up and round into a sitting position, roughly pushing away Dimitar's hands. 'What do you really want?'

'I want what I've always wanted.' Boris folded his arms. 'Didn't we both want the same things? Everybody does. We disagreed fundamentally about how to bring it about. I was a child of my time, Feliks. As you were of yours. Now Time has proved you right, and me wrong. We were on opposite sides once. But now there's only one possible side. Feliks, I have my faults, but stupidity is not one of them.'

This at least was the truth. His father was possibly the most intelligent man he had ever met. In his early teenage years Feliks had basked in the reflected glory of his father's authority, admiring his wit and self-assertion, relishing the power of his surname, the effect of it on teachers at school who would otherwise have punished his crazy, disrespectful behaviour . . .

Dimitar's fingers pressed down on his shoulders. He didn't shrug them off.

'I can see that the new ways are fragile,' Boris continued,

'Like any newborn baby, they must be nurtured and protected from . . .'

'Protected from people who still think the way you used to? Or perhaps from people who still think the way *I* used to? What do you really want? D'you want me to contact all my old idealistic companions and induce them to crawl out of the woods for you, so that the new freedoms will be less fragile? You'll get nothing from me. I've seen no one.'

'I'm not . . .'

'I don't know where anyone is. I don't even know how we won. I was dead, remember?'

'That was one of the first things that struck me,' his father smoothed back his hair, in a gesture Feliks remembered well, a gesture he had practised as a boy, wanting to be like his father, wanting to be him. 'There you were, on the brink of the old way's ending, and you didn't live to see it. You'll have to watch the old news reports and you can . . .'

'You're wasting your time! I can't tell you anything you don't . . .'

'Who is the legitimate ruler of our country?'

Feliks stared at him. The word 'legitimate' was meaningless in any world that Boris inhabited. 'I've no idea,' he said.

'What about the Archduke Stephanos?'

'Stephanos? I believe he died. Like me. But long ago, and more permanently.'

'His great-grand-daughter Irina is alive and well.'

'Good. I'm happy for her.'

'She's living in England.'

'A wonderful country. Not as wonderful as home, of course.'

'I hope you will convince her of that. I am surrounded by self-serving idiots, and I don't intend to watch this country die before it has a chance to live. You are the last honest man, Feliks. I want you go to England and bring back our Countess.'

The same attendant was waiting to guide him out, but they took a different route, into a different room, one with modern showers. When the man diffidently suggested Feliks might like to use them, out of spite he shook his head. He had left Tavcaryevna in his vestments but now they were nowhere to be seen. Underwear of good quality was waiting for him, still in plastic wrappers, neatly stacked on a table. Several shirts and three suits hung on a metal rail. All in his size. A choice of socks. And shoes, again, all in his size. He'd never worn shoes like these in his life. Butter-soft leather. Italian. They even smelled expensive. Some minion had done his homework well.

He got dressed, then considered himself in the wall mirror. But the man who looked back was not him. That was not his face. The left eye was narrow, distorted by a thin ragged line that ran from the temple all the way into the dark beard. The nose was wrong too. He stood motionless, mesmerised, appalled.

Chapter Eight

'Dina, my angel, I believe I've left the disc for the Hamiltons in the kitchen,' Irene held out her house keys, 'and stupidly, I don't have a copy. If you go now, you'll be back well before they come in. No need to run, just don't stop to smell all the roses.'

'How long have I got?'

'Half an hour tops.'

She could have said forty-five minutes, but that would become an hour. You had to allow Dina a little 'distraction time'. Apart from this minor flaw, she really was an angel, Irene mused, turning back to the task in hand. No job too trivial, an excellent finder of lost objects, able to anticipate a person's needs and understand their moods. Terribly indecisive if not kept busy and clearly directed though. She'd driven Paul crazy on the odd occasion when Ronni had been unwell, and Dina had been lent to him.

'You just have to be very clear and very specific,' she'd told him.

'How do you cope?'

'I'm very clear and very specific. You've been spoiled.'

'By Ronni?'

'By everyone in this building, darling.'

They were like a perfect salad dressing, Paul had once told her. He was the oil, and she was the vinegar. An expensive balsamic. A Paltrinieri, he said, or something like it.

She sighed and pulled out another sample book. Sometimes it was best to go back to the old favourites when an idea refused to develop. She was so tired of black, despite clients still wanting it. The Hamiltons had a wonderful top floor, and still they were reluctant to let go of black leather. Or grey, they said. She was tireder still of grey. Every year she dreaded winter. Grey skies and often pale grey at that, they depressed her so much.

'You'll be living here in winter too,' she'd told the Hamiltons. But they were accountants, both of them, not a creative bone in their desperately rational bodies. They didn't even seem able to make the, to all intents and purposes rational, leap between paying her lots of money and accepting her advice. They were passionate about trees, they said, that was one fixed point. She'd incorporated stylized branches into the wet room, and developed them in more muted tones on the walls in the master bedroom. They'd liked the leaf designs on the dining table, and the chair frames, but she was going to have to break it to them soon that there could be too much of a good thing.

Dina, in complete contrast, was delightful, a little, biddable sponge, soaking up all the knowledge and advice she could.

'It's huge, isn't it?' she'd said in her first week.

'Design? Of course,' Irene had told her, amused and pleased. 'It's the Universe. It's all there is.'

She was pleased because Dina had taken it all on board so quickly – the mystery of creativity, its irrationality, its connection to the indefinable personality of the artist. She had a good instinctive sense of colour. Whether she would ever go deeper was another question. She was a bit of a butterfly, sipping from this flower and that, not always pausing to think too deeply. Subjectivity and profound thoughts were not Dina's style. Her childhood had apparently been idyllic, and her life, Irene thought, would be a happy one, since it would consist of looking after other people, and there would never be a shortage of people who wanted to be looked after.

She almost envied Dina. Her own childhood had been quite different. Born far too late in her parents' marriage, tolerated by a father who spent his life listening to grand opera and dwelling on what might have been, and a mother who continued to drown her past and present sorrows in the most genteel fashion. Neither had tried to understand her at all. For a time in her teens she had wondered if she might have been adopted, she was so unlike either of them.

She glanced at the wall board. The Zoological Society had sent a handwritten letter of thanks for her help with the auction several weeks earlier, which was rather sweet of them. *These animals have no obvious benefit to humans. No vested interests will attempt to save them.*

She despised people who looked on the natural world as something to be used. They were, she felt, merely a small step away from people who felt the same about other people. Nor was it enough to love tigers and pandas: their charisma attracted everyone. They were exciting and fun. Whereas, if you believed that all species had an inherent right to exist, it hurt to read of guinea pigs in Brazil (down to 40 individuals), tortoises in Madagascar, silky lemurs and sandcats, hunted, killed by fire, driven out by human expansion.

She'd been driven out in her late teens by her father's indifference. It had taken her a long time to realise that this was not because there was something wrong in her, and to understand also that her mother's alternating kindness and cruelty depended on whim, rather than anything she herself did or failed to do. There was no logic in it. She could have a bad report from school and be assured that spelling didn't matter, and be comforted with chocolate, then come home with a good report for something else, maths, say, which wouldn't elicit praise, because 'You won't need it. We use calculators now, darling.'

When they went out, they went out together, leaving her with a neighbour, who wanted to watch tv programmes she was too young to watch and made her go to bed too early. She'd decided at the age of seven never to pluck her eyebrows, since the woman had said, 'You've got nice hair, Irene, but you'll have to do something with those when you're older.'

Her first affair had been a huge step forward in so many ways, not hampered one bit by her apparently wayward eyebrows. It had ended in tears, but she had emerged stronger (too naïve to know that this was an established cliché) and with a new set of rules. Different didn't mean wrong. Knowing what you wanted was good. The easily available was not all that appealing. Regret could be sweet, but was best kept short. And in some instances, regret was pointless. She hadn't gone to her father's funeral, and she hadn't tortured herself about it. Torturing yourself about what had happened or not happened was only interesting up to a point.

She looked at the sofa designs again. She'd never tortured herself about leather either. Sheep, goats and cows were not endangered. She hadn't used a lot of leather at the Bank, because the brief had suggested some of their clients were sensitive about it. A great pity, but you had to follow the brief. It had been quite an anxious time. Too many people wanting to put in their tuppence worth, was how Paul had put it. She'd felt her confidence beginning to dissipate halfway through, which was just a little scary, so she'd handed it over to him. Paul was better with Corporate clients. She herself was too different from the unthinking masses to handle their world with patience.

Blue was what the Hamiltons needed. She would sell it to them as a grey, but in their well-lit expanse, it would be blue.

Chapter Nine

Still no comment on her hair. Was it possible Irene hadn't noticed that she'd become a blonde overnight? Well, not completely blond. It was a trial run, and would wash out after a while. It marked the one month anniversary of goodbye to Derek. Derek who'd admired her 'sweet round face'. Deodorant Derek, the man with the most fragrant armpits in town. Fragrant armpits, she realised now, were not what she craved in a man.

The disc would probably not be in Irene's kitchen. Like many creative people, Irene frequently lost track of where things were, and it was frequently Dina's job to find them. She paused in the office corridor to look again at a photograph, cut from Interior Design Today. Irene from the waist up, sitting in a row of designers at the annual one day conference, elegant as always, her hair pinned up with one of the fabulous clasps she had inherited from her aristocratic ancestors.

She gave a little sigh. She herself was a peasant. Stocky fishermen and crofters and the odd Viking marauder had provided her with no innate elegance whatsoever. At least her legs were good. Lots of small women had fattish legs. And tall women too. Irene's legs were fattish. Well, not fat. But not terribly slim. Dina glanced down. Slim ankles. Very satisfactory.

Outside, the sun was pleasantly warm. She liked Glasgow's West End. There were so many mature trees, it was almost like a stroll in the country, if you ignored the traffic noise. Irene's flat was only a twenty minute walk, and quite a few of the curving streets had big, well-tended 'residents only' gardens surrounded by railings, with colour and scents and birdsong for peasants walking by to enjoy.

Not that she deserved to be loved for her ankles alone. And not that finding a man was the sole purpose of her life. It was just proving harder than she had anticipated. 'You have to kiss a lot of frogs,' someone had reminded her once, 'before you find your prince.' Did other girls have to kiss as many as she did? And why could she never spot the frogs in advance?

Everyone seemed happy to be out today. It was almost autumn but people were still wearing summer clothes. She loved being in the heart of the city. A place of her own would be better than having to share. She was saving the income from the croft, more or less, and maybe some day there would be enough for a deposit for something. Although Rachel who owned the flat was really nice. She was a social worker who also made cakes for parties so there were sometimes tasting sessions.

She loved her job: colours and textures, the history and theory, the buzz of multiple new things from all around the globe happening all around her. Of course she only had a little corner separated by a wall of glass bricks from Irene's big office, but as soon as she sat down in the morning and switched on the laptop, she felt needed. She felt like someone who could become capable, given time. By which she meant not just capable at her job, which she felt she was already, but capable at life generally. She liked Paul, and his two trainees, Oliver and Jonah, and Ronni, his PA, who together turned Irene's inspired ideas into reality. There was a quiet man who did mysterious things upstairs on a computer and never smiled back when they passed on the stairs. Ronni was the one she felt most at ease with. She and Ronni often had fun lunches together. Ronni was in her mid-forties, originally from America with British citizenship through her Scottish mother. She wore her curly hair very short and very white and had for a period in her life been an anarchist. 'But I was never violent,' she said, 'because my Daddy was in the CIA and though I wanted to embarrass him, I was kinda cautious.'

Before meeting Ronni, she'd never given anarchy a thought. Nursing College in Inverness hadn't dwelt on it, nor had her other admin jobs. It was about freeing the individual, and finding your true self, Ronni said.

The houses here probably didn't have a lot of anarchists in them, she thought. They had walls or high privet front hedges so you couldn't see in. But there were flowers growing freely along most of the walls, being their true selves. She stopped for a sniff at some yellow roses, wishing she could keep the scent inside her. So faint but so beautiful. Elusive. That was the word.

She had to stand still to let an elderly man cycle across in front of her. Bad man, she chided him silently. No helmet. She had cycled to school, always with a helmet on. Her father had insisted. The island's roads weren't busy outside the tourist season, but they were always dangerous, because the wind could level you like a blow from a hockey stick at any time of the year, and because no local ever slowed down and because sheep were too stupid to move out of your way, especially if the tarmac was dry and warmer than their field.

It was a really lovely day. She slipped off her cardigan, and put it in her capacious handbag. Canvas with leather trim. She was learning to trust her own taste. Ronni had told her, 'Never do what everybody else does without thinking.'

45

A middle-aged woman with a border terrier in a red harness smiled at her in a friendly way as they passed. More sensible than a collar, kinder to the dog. 'Love, joy, peace, patience, kindness.' She still remembered the list from Sunday school, more or less. She liked that about Glasgow. Complete strangers were often friendly.

The two middle-aged women in the showroom downstairs weren't kind or friendly, but then as Ronni said, 'Upstairs and downstairs, honey. Everyone's different. It's their problem.' They were apparently really nice to the customers. Possibly they'd decided that being their true selves involved being free to dislike other people without cause.

Irene maintained her freedom. She had never lived with a male friend. 'We're such opposites,' she had said of one. 'He likes the toilet roll to unroll that way,' she'd gestured with both hands, 'and I like it to unroll this way.'

That couldn't be the real reason, Dina thought. What kind of people cared which way the toilet roll unrolled? It wasn't something she'd ever noticed. That might be part of her problem. Not knowing what she wanted exactly. Perhaps Irene was right. Perhaps what made relationships last was knowing what you wanted in even the small things. Being decisive. She tried to walk more decisively but gave up. It wasn't easy in heels on an uneven pavement. Shoes were so much easier for men, like everything else.

The fine weather had brought out lots of mothers with babies, as if they'd been hatching over the summer. Some day, possibly, she thought. Loads of time. No one she knew had babies. Not that she would mind making babies with the right man. For the right man, she would make babies till the cows came home.

The hallway of Irene's basement flat was just as she remembered it, constricted on both sides by shelves of books, valuable objets d'art, curious bits of faded writing under glass, and paintings, large and small, of Irene's aristocratic ancestors, who had arrived in Britain as fugitives from somewhere in Europe. It wasn't cluttered, Irene wouldn't be able to function amidst clutter, it was just very full of stuff in comparison with the rest of the public rooms, which were sparingly furnished. It was, she thought, kind of the opposite way from most people's homes, which were easy to get into and cluttered as you got further in.

'Bebe?' she called cautiously, before going any further. 'Nice cat? Bebe?'

In truth, Bebe was *not* a nice cat. A large, un-neutered lilac point show Siamese, with bright blue eyes and a vicious temper, he adored Irene as much as he loathed the rest of humanity. Irene wouldn't accept any criticism, though. Bebe could turn taps on and off, enjoyed watching the ten o'clock news and only talked when he had something interesting to say. Paul had been heard to comment that the cat was very beautiful but 'too smart for his own good'.

She walked cautiously down the long corridor, eyeing the tops of the shelves and the ceiling lights. At one of Irene's elegant Sunday brunches, she had seen Bebe with bared claws drop like Attila's wrath from the sitting room curtains onto the neck of a man who choked on his canapé and vomited.

There was no sign of Bebe in the sitting room. The crimson leather sofa was cat-free, as were the long curtains at the French windows, heavy gold and black brocade, the ones Irene intended to be buried in, since they had cost so much. Irene had broken all the rules in this room, mixing different reds, dark blues and golds, and art from different eras. The effect was spellbinding.

Enough of this, she told herself. Disc for the Hamiltons.

She had to push to get the kitchen door open. There was a large sports bag stuck behind it.

'I'm so sorry. Was that in your way?'

The man who spoke was standing by the sink, washing his hands. He didn't sound like a workman, though he was wearing overalls.

'I'm sorry,' he repeated. 'We're here to check the washing machine. The door wasn't locked, so we came in. Are you the homeowner? Miss Arbanisi?'

'No. I work for her. But I had to unlock it,' she said. He had gorgeous eyes, almost as blue as Bebe's.

'Did you? That's odd. I've been trying to phone you. I mean her. But she's not picking up. We were supposed to meet here.'

'Were you trying the office or her mobile?'

Before he could say anything, another man came in right behind her.

'Dan, this young lady works for the homeowner. I've just explained that we're here to fix this old bugger.' He gave the washing machine a thump.

The big man said nothing. He wore the same navy overalls as the other, with a picture in gold of a leaky tap and spanner above the breast pocket.

'Reliable most of the time, this model, but when they break down, they really break down,' the first man said.

The front door bell rang.

'That might be her,' Dina said, though she realised it made no sense for Irene to be ringing her own bell. Especially since the door wasn't locked. The bell rang again, this time as if someone was leaning on it.

'Why would she be ringing the bell?' the big man asked.

'The door's not locked,' she said. It might be someone returning the cat, she supposed, if he'd bolted when the workmen came it. He wasn't supposed to go out at all.

'Let's both go,' said the other. 'Dan, could you try that phone number again?'

48

He put his hand on her back as they went through the sitting room, as if she needed help. It wasn't all that annoying, barely touching. *Be reasonable* she told herself as they made their way to the door. *Everybody's different. He doesn't mean anything.*

Chapter Ten

'Miss Arbanisi? Irina Arbanisi?'

The man asking the question was looking closely at her. He had ugly scars all down one side of his face. There was another man behind him facing the row of steps up to the street.

'I'm not . . .' she began, stopping when the plumber gave her a little squeeze. She moved, quite sure now she didn't want his arm around her waist, but back it came, and now there was nowhere to move to.

'I need to talk with you, if I may. The matter is complex.'

He sounded foreign. His dark hair and beard were neatly trimmed, but there was no getting away from the scars.

The plumber said, 'Sorry, this isn't a good time. We're very busy.'

'If this is not a good time, I will return. Perhaps you would prefer also to have my telephone number . . .'

'Sorry, pal.'

The plumber pushed the door shut. Confused, Dina followed him back into the sitting room, but went towards the window, wanting to see what the two men would do next. She tripped on something behind the armchair, looked down and screamed.

The man called Dan came running.

'It's Bebe,' she screamed again.

The other one came and caught hold of her hand, 'It's

all right, it's all right,' he began. She heard the other say, 'Bloody stupid name for a cat, though.'

There was a loud reverberating bang. Instantly, the man dropped her hand. The two of them rushed towards the hall, to reappear seconds later, moving backwards, struggling with the bearded man and his lighter haired friend. The friend was locked round the big man's middle, all of them bashing about into the chairs and the coffee table. The standard lamp fell over. Stumbling, half-crawling, she got past them. She'd left her bag in the kitchen, but the house phone was nearer, a ridiculous ornate cream and gilt thing, slippery in her shaking fingers. She'd just managed to dial the numbers, and say a few words when the friend and the fat plumber came crashing into her, then back into the middle of the sitting room, rolling across the floor and smashing into the beautiful butterscotch leather Blava chair. The dark bearded one got to his feet, yelling gibberish at her. She dropped the phone and ran into Irene's bedroom. There wasn't a lock. She braced herself against it. There was a mighty yell, several, a loud crack, another massive thump. And silence.

Her legs collapsed and she slid to a sitting position on the carpet. Voices. One, then someone else replying. The first voice louder. Silence again. She looked about her. Nowhere to hide.

'Miss Arbanisi. Please to come out.'

She didn't. The request was made again. There was no other noise. Shaking, she opened the door a fraction. She saw the handsome plumber first, on his back, not moving. The bearded scarred man was crouching down beside the fat one at the other side of the room. The man at the door was beckoning her forward, nervously holding out his hand, talking to her in a language she didn't understand.

Chapter Eleven

'It's all right. You're safe. The danger's over,' Lazslo said, holding out his hand. The girl wouldn't take it.

Feliks looked over. So this was their Countess. What a superb beginning. In less than ten minutes they'd managed to reduce the country's future monarch to a shaking terrified girl under a bush of dishevelled blond hair.

Getting to his feet, he swore loudly.

'What did you want me to do, for fuck's sake?' Lazslo snapped back. 'He had a knife. He was going to kill me.'

'You could have hit him somewhere peripheral once you got it from him.'

'Oh, I'm sorry, I should have told him to stand still and give me a chance to stab him gently. Besides, it was peripheral. He's not nearly dead.'

Feliks looked at the Arbanisi girl. All colour had drained from her face. They'd seen from her face at the door that something was wrong, but the scream had decided it. Once in, there was no time to think, no option but to fight them, whoever they were.

They didn't have much time. The smaller one wasn't going to stay asleep for long. He moved towards the girl.

'Don't be frightened,' he began, in English, for it seemed her command of her native language was rusty or non-existent. 'We aren't going to hurt you. What are these men?'

She stared at him, grey eyes wide. Her eye make-up had dribbled all over her face.

'Are they dead?'

'No. They will be waking soon.'

'They said they'd come to fix the washing machine.'

This meant nothing. He let it pass.

'We are from the old country, Miss Arbanisi. We are here to ask you to . . .'

'I phoned the police . . . they won't be long.'

'You want to phone the police?'

'No, I already did. They'll be here soon. I told them where to come.'

He called to Lazslo, who'd been checking the rest of the rooms. He appeared at once in the doorway.

'We have to go. She called the police.'

'Let's go then,' Lazslo said, 'Your fellow is just as bad as mine, by the way. I think you hit him in a very sore place. Also, he has driving licences and bank cards in several names.'

'Really?'

'All English names. You want them?'

'No.'

Feliks turned back to the girl, 'This is all a very big mistake. We have to go. But we must come back. We can explain everything. You must say to the police . . .' but what was she to say to the police?

'I don't . . . this . . . this is *insane* . . . who *are* you people anyway? I don't . . .' Her voice faded. He caught her just before she hit the floor.

'Oh, shit,' Lazslo said.

Feliks shifted his stance. She was heavier than she looked.

'Get the car started.'

'We're not taking her, are we?'

'Well, we're sure as hell not leaving her with them.'

53

Chapter Twelve

He carried her out to the car and angled her into the rear seat. This was all wrong. If she hadn't phoned the police, there would have been time to think, time to get things straight in his head. Now everything was completely haywire.

Her legs were good, but her skirt was too short, and quite tawdry. Her clothes were in fact rather tasteless, he felt. One would have to admit that her breasts were full and well-rounded but she wasn't as beautiful as her photograph, nor as elegant. Ah well, he supposed even a Countess might have an off day.

There were people in the street, but no one seemed to be paying attention. He fastened her seat belt, then got into the front seat beside Lazslo.

'Where to?' Lazslo asked, accelerating carefully.

'Back to the cottage.'

'So nothing's changed.'

'Is that meant to be a joke?'

He felt Lazslo flinch and was tempted to slap him. Instead he forced himself to bite down hard on his anger.

This at least was something Lazslo could be trusted to do safely, he thought, watching the steady hands on the wheel. Lazslo had always understood machines, from bicycles to paddle steamers. The inner workings of computers held no mysteries for him. He handled cars well, and he knew how to fix them. Better for him if he'd never left Kocevje.

He'd have been a prosperous mechanic by now, living quietly above his own garage, with a fleet of three shiny taxis and nothing to be anxious about but carburettors and brake pads. With no opportunity for grand ideas. No opportunity to mix with the rich and powerful and sell his soul and stab strangers in the belly.

'What's wrong?' Laszlo asked.

'Nothing. Watch the road.' He tried to say it calmly. Who were those men and why?

The shopkeepers in this country seemed to be addicted to perverse spelling. *Krazy Kuts*, he read. Then further on, *Trendz Fashion Clothes* in jagged black letters on a luminous green background. *What Everyone Wants* said another.

'Promise our Countess whatever she wants,' Boris had told him. 'If she doesn't want glory, offer her money. Tell her about the estates. Offer her a mountain lodge in Celovska. Just bring her back.'

So were those men working for Boris? It was surely too much of a coincidence that they had been at the house precisely when he and Lazslo arrived. And was Lazslo to be trusted? He'd been working for Janek all these years. Whose orders was he obeying now? How much did Lazslo know that he wasn't telling? He hated this. How could you fight your enemies if you didn't know who they were?

There was movement in the back seat. She was awake, trying to get the door open.

'No, don't do that. You're safe . . .' he began.

Now she was screaming, thumping on the window with both hands. Distracted, Laszlo swerved. His cigarette fell from his lips. He brushed frantically at his lap. Behind them a horn sounded. He'd been stupid, Feliks saw. He should have anticipated this, should have sat beside her. He threw off his safety belt, and lunging over between the seats managed to grab first one wrist then the other.

'Be still,' he said. This time he remembered to speak English, repeating it over and over, more and more gently until at last she stopped struggling.

'We are on *your* side,' he told her.

'If you're going to rape me, go ahead, but you'll have to kill me too, because once I get away from. . . .'

'Nobody's going to hurt you.'

'Yes you are, you're just saying that you want me to behave so nobody out there thinks there's anything wrong, you must think I'm a complete fool I don't know who those men were I've nothing worth stealing and nobody would pay a ransom for me so it's pretty obvious you're only after one thing. . . .'

What lungs she must have! Like an elephant!

'Miss Arbanisi, I promise you, if anyone ever rapes you, it will not be me. We were sent here to. . . .'

'Let go, you're *hurting*. And I'm . . .'

'If you only calm down, I will let go. There is no point in . . .'

'. . . *not* Irene! I was only getting something for her because she's too busy with a client, and she'll be wondering where. . . .'

'What are you saying?'

'What d'you mean what am I saying?'

She met his eyes for the first time.

'Don't make a joke of this,' he said, 'it's not a time for joking.'

'You think I'm having fun?'

'Why do you deny who you are?'

'Because I'm not her. I'm not Irene.'

He dropped her wrists. 'Then who are you?' He shot a

56

look at Lazslo, who protested at once, in their own tongue, 'The address was right. She's trying to . . .'

'Shut up! Find somewhere to stop.'

'What?'

'You heard me.' He turned back round to her. 'So who the hell *are* you?'

She was crying again.

'You're *not* Irina Arbanisi?'

'I just told you. I work for her. She was too busy. How many times have I got to tell you?'

They pulled into a lane between two houses. Lazslo switched off the engine.

'You don't believe this crap, do you?' he said. 'She's scared witless by what happened. She's obviously lying.'

'Does she look like a princess to you? When I was a child, I had a picture book with several of them in it. They generally wore long white dresses and had gold tiaras on their heads.' He looked at their passenger in the mirror. 'I'm beginning to think we've got ourselves a peasant by mistake.'

'Are you talking about me?' the girl said.

'Yes,' he told her, in English.

'What are you saying?'

'We can't decide whether to give you the poison apple now, or leave you for the wild animals in the depths of the nearest forest,' he told her.

'Who are you? Why do you want Irene?'

'I can't tell you. Unless you're her. If you were her, I could explain everything.'

He watched her face in the mirror.

'Who were those men if they weren't plumbers?' she said.

'You tell me. They were in your house.'

'It's *not* my house. I don't know why any of this is

57

happening. So you can open the bloody door and let me out.'

'And what will you tell the police?' he asked.

She pushed her hair back from her face and wiped at her eyes with the back of her hand, spreading the black marks further. He bit back a smile.

'I won't go to the police.'

'You won't have to. They will come to you.'

This made her pause.

'They don't know it was me. I didn't give my name, In fact I'm not even sure I got through . . . there's actually no way they could . . . Oh shit.'

'Shit?'

'My bag.'

His heart sank, although this possibility had already occurred to him. He'd not seen a handbag, but every woman carried one. He'd been a fool not to look for it.

'Then you see the difficulty. When the police find your bag, they will come to you.'

'I'll tell them I . . . I'll say I went in and found those men in the flat. And I thought they were plumbers. But then I found Bebe, and I screamed, and you were passing and came in to help. I phoned the police, and then I ran away.'

'And then they will look for us. You will describe us.'

'No, I won't. I'll say it was all too quick. I ran out as soon as I made the phone call. I'll tell them I hardly saw either of you. But now I've calmed down, so I should phone the police. So the best thing would be to let me go, right now. So *I* can phone *them* before they look for me.'

She had a brain then. She was trying to think, to her credit, despite her clown's face and wild hair. Should he risk letting her go? If she was telling the truth and she wasn't Miss Arbanisi, she could be persuaded to arrange a

58

meeting with the real one. There was an office, of course, but he'd decided to avoid it as being too public.

'How long are we going to sit here?' Lazslo asked.

'Till I tell you to move.'

'All right. Whatever you want. I thought I'd mention something, but never mind, I won't.'

'Tell me.'

'Nothing much, really. Just that red BMW beside the bread shop over there. Dark-haired man. Denim shirt.'

'You think he's interested in us?'

'Could be.'

'Why didn't you say sooner?'

'I wasn't sure.'

'Let's go. Let him get close enough so we can see his face, then lose him.'

Chapter Thirteen

Charles John De Bono stared at the fine plasterwork of the sitting room ceiling. Was he alone? There were no sounds except the quiet noise of traffic in the street. The side of his face ached, but the pain in his groin was excruciating, as if some heavily-built animal, a rhino possibly, had used it as a footstool.

He lay still, trying to recollect what had happened. A girl who wasn't the owner of the flat. Two foreigners who thought she was. He got himself into a sitting position, then to his feet, but very slowly, leaning on the wall until the room levelled out. He checked his pockets. Everything was as it should be. Wallet, keys, diary.

Not quite alone. Here was Dan, bleeding on the rather lovely carpet, refusing to wake up. What an idiot. Stabbed with his own knife. Since he didn't seem inclined to wake up, it would be an act of kindness to help him on his way. A mere act of kindness. Charles took one of the velvet cushions from the sofa and held it down hard on Dan's face for as long as it took. Then carefully picking up the knife with his own handkerchief, he walked to the kitchen, lifted the girl's handbag from the worktop, slipped the knife into it and the whole lot into his holdall wherein lay the few small precious items they'd collected before the interruption. He exited through the door to the garden, and delicately made his way, legs well apart, to the car in the back lane.

He drove ever so courteously for the next ten minutes

or so, making a point of breathing, and giving way to everything in his path, deaf-blind middle-aged women in cars too big for them, cretins in delivery vans and anorexic cyclists, both male and female. He had no clue where he was going, but it didn't much matter. What mattered was avoiding sudden movements of any kind. As soon as he saw a space, he pulled in and stopped. After a while he managed to put a bit of chewing gum into his mouth and loosen the top two buttons of his overalls. Being a burglar, he thought, was not going to suit him. Worth a try, and interesting in its own way, but not for him. Essentially it required manual skills he did not possess, forcing him to rely on morons like Dan, who promised he could quickly open safes but could not in fact do so. The Dans of this world were in fact so irreparably inept the world was better off without them. He was seriously pissed off, but since it was always sensible to be pissed off at a safe distance from any given situation, as soon as he could bear it, he moved into the traffic again.

After meandering along a little more, he saw a Tesco sign and turned into a crowded car park, finding a space on the roof. He got the seat back as far as it went, took off the overalls, combed his hair and put on a tie and the suit jacket which had lain on the back seat. In the pharmacy he begged for the strongest painkiller they could give him, blaming root canal treatment. *Just something to get me home.* The girl saw his face, felt his pain and took pity. She wouldn't tell him what the tablet was, made him promise to tell no one, and gave him water to swallow it. Back in the car he sat for a while watching pigeons, clouds, the populace come and go. Noticing a few cream-coloured cat hairs on his trouser leg, he removed them carefully. The animal had tried to scratch him. It had been the work of a moment to end its life. Mostly he was indifferent to animals. Some were of course necessary for food. But when he found himself considering the existence of pets, which in truth he rarely did, he was mystified by people's need for them.

Holiday? he wondered. He had travelled a lot recently, but always on business. The idea of a holiday had its charms. There were still quite a few countries he'd never been to. In the past year he'd set himself a challenge, trying new things, or 'callings', as he liked to call them. He'd been an antiques dealer very briefly in the early days, and Miss Arbanisi's auction items, advertised on the net, had re-awakened the attraction. And he'd always liked a trip up to Scotland. The people were very trusting. A little research had indicated a house full of valuables, on the ground floor, no alarm system, the owner out at work all day, but really, on reflection, being a burglar wasn't meeting his needs as much as he'd hoped.

As the pain began to fade, his mind began to work again. He hated being bored, and it was such fun tidying loose ends. The girl first. He emptied the contents of her bag on the passenger seat. A cardigan, a purse with some notes and coins, about fifteen pounds or so. Nothing much else. Keys, credit cards in the name of Donaldina MacLeod. A packet of anti-diarrhoea capsules. He hoped she wasn't needing them at the moment, wherever she was. A tube of hand-sanitising gel. Used paper handkerchiefs. Hair brush, rather unpleasant, as full of hair. A bulging make-up bag – he didn't even open that. Mobile phone. Excellent. He kept this and the hand gel, shovelled the rest back in.

The foreigners were next on the list. They thought she was the house owner. Her screams had brought them back. So, they didn't know her, but the real owner was impor-tant to them. Who were they and what had they come for? Was it important to know or not? Had they all scarpered together? What was the best way to track them down?

Charles doodled in his head around a large question mark, adding jagged little lines.

In front of him a young couple were stowing their shopping bags in the boot of their car. The man looked tired, his mouth turned down at the corners. The girl wore a white halter top that threatened to unload its contents at any moment. Why were young women so determined to show their boobs? It didn't interest him one way or the other, but he'd heard some men complain that there was no mystery any more, no subtlety. He'd been in a few church groups, during his very enjoyable 'born again' periods, and even there, women were now going as far as they could go. Things in churches were changing to quite a disturbing extent. What a lot of hugging he'd had to go through the last time. And handkerchiefs. That was another thing. It seemed hardly any men his age carried cloth handkerchiefs. He'd quickly realised the usefulness of keeping a clean one in his pocket for tears during powerful hymns and sermons. He'd invested in various monogrammed ones. Women found it reassuring that there were faithful if rather dull female relatives somewhere buying him gifts. *No, keep it please,* had been one of his most productive lines. Easy money, church groups, but too predictable after a while.

His phone let out a little beep. Mother's birthday the following Wednesday. He wrote 'Interflora' on Monday's space. If he forgot she would become a nuisance, telling complete strangers how neglected she was. It wasn't even true. He paid for her car, her rent and her fuel bills. It was a small price to pay to keep the bitch completely out of his life. She had emphysema, but refused to shuffle off her mortal coil. He angled the mirror and studied his face. There might or might not be a bruise.

'What big eyes you have, Mister Wolf,' he told himself.

63

Chapter Fourteen

Fear is a good thing, Dina told herself as they passed through several small villages with names she didn't recognise. *Fear is an ancient instinct. Only machines fear nothing.* Someone had said that in a lecture. *Allow your patients to find out what they fear and what they value, no matter how different your values may be.*

There was a long unpopulated stretch of countryside, till they finally left the main road to drive up a deserted lane. Her head felt as tight as a balloon on the point of bursting.

It was cool inside the car. Air conditioning she supposed. The two of them had jackets on, but her arms were cold, and rubbing them didn't help. Someone had told her not so long ago that she was brave, she couldn't remember who, but it was utterly, utterly not true. *I fear being killed. I value staying alive,* she thought. She'd watched enough TV to know that the fact they hadn't blindfolded her was not good, since it meant they intended to kill her in the end.

She looked around. Fields without animals. A medium-sized rocky hill on the left. Birch trees on either side, but no dark and lonely wood. In films there was generally a dark and lonely wood. The scary one with the scarred face would strangle her of course, but when she was found, his blood would be under her nails, and a strand of her hair on his clothes. A nice young couple in green wellies out walking with a friendly, pink-tongued black Labrador puppy would stumble over her decomposing body . . .

'Out,' he told her, unlocking her door.

The only building in sight was a small cottage surrounded by an overgrown garden. Inside, it smelled of
damp carpet and fried bacon. Her heart was outdoing
itself. Probably it would burst before her head did. She sat
down on a faded sofa in front of a fireplace where logs had
long ago burned down to ashes. The surface of the glass-
topped coffee table was grey with dust. Someone had put
daisies and buttercups in a small green glass bottle, but the
water had dried away, leaving the flowers stiff and faded.

'I need to pee,' she said.

'You wish to use the bathroom?' It was the nervous,
good-looking one.

'Actually, I wish to go home,' she said.

He looked worried, and she wondered for a split second
if he was wishing for the same thing.

'You are not in danger here,' he said. 'This place is good
for you.'

Clearly his ideas about danger and goodness were completely different from hers, she thought, as she hovered
above the toilet, touching the lever afterwards through a
wad of paper. All of which caution was ridiculous, because
she would be dead soon enough, raped and most probably
infected with some unspeakable foreign disease into the
bargain . . .

There was one piece of purple soap and a chewed looking nail brush. On the window ledge lay several skeletal
bluebottles, and a contorted tube of toothpaste with no
cap. The cupboard held a few towels, a box of Man-size
Kleenex, and a bottle of White Musk shower gel that
smelled foul.

Face your fear and it will go away. She saw her face in
the dusty mirror over the sink, and didn't know whether to
laugh or cry. Then she knew, and cried. No wonder they

hadn't wanted to look at her. There was no hot water, but with the Kleenex she cleaned up the best she could.

The nervous man jumped up from the sofa when she came back into the main room. The ugly one was nowhere to be seen.

'You are cold?' he asked. 'I will make a fire. Or perhaps first I make coffee. Or tea. You prefer the tea? Soon you can go home,' he added 'Very soon. I'm sorry.'

He really did look sorry. Perhaps that was what all the arguing had been about in the car. He wanted to let her go, and the ugly one didn't.

'Why are you keeping me here?' she said.

'I have no choice.'

'I won't tell anyone about you. You could let me go. While he's not here.'

'I . . . we do not hurt you. It is for your safety.'

'I know *you* won't hurt me. You're not like him, you . . .'

'Don't let those big blue eyes fool you. Lazslo is just as cruel and depraved as I am.'

How long had he been standing in the doorway? He was carrying a pile of logs which he let fall in front of the fireplace.

'What is your name?' he said.

'Dina MacLeod.'

'Deena? That is an English name?'

It was Scottish. Scottish at its worst Highland excess. Donaldina, the first girl in the family for years in an unbroken line of males.

He didn't wait for her answer, but turned his back and began to stack the wood. 'I am Feliks Berisovic Albescu,' he said, as if it meant something.

'I was going to light the fire. Shall I make coffee?' the nervous one said. 'There is also cake. It is called a carrot cake. It is very pleasant.'

Was she going mad, or were they? She'd just been kidnapped and now they wanted her to have coffee and carrot cake?

'You said before that you work for Miss Arbanisi.' The ugly one straightened, wiping his hands on his trousers. 'Does that mean you can contact her?'

'You mean phone her?'

'The phone would be best. Our last carrier pigeon died this morning.'

'Your what?'

'I believe it ate some of the cake. Do you have her number?'

'My mobile's in my bag.'

'There is no reception here,' the nervous one said. 'Too many hills.'

'I know the number, and the office number,' she said. 'If she's still there.'

The ugly one looked at his watch and frowned. 'Then we had better not waste time,' he said. 'There is a public telephone box on the road. It's not far.'

Chapter Fifteen

Outside the shadows had already begun to lengthen. There was no pavement and at first Feliks tried to help the girl by supporting her elbow as they walked along the rough grass verge, but she pulled away from him.

'What d'you think I'm going to do, run away?' she muttered.

She went on muttering, at some length, but he paid scant attention. He had to get it right this time. He had to choose exactly the right words.

She wobbled and he caught her.

'Why do you wear such shoes if you cannot walk in them?'

'I can walk in them. I just can't *run* in them,' she announced, and with a defiant lift of the chin, she moved onto the tarmac, marching ahead of him, the tightly-encased bottom swaying from side to side.

The small space inside the phone booth smelled of cigarette butts and urine, exactly like those at home. He gave her some coins, let her dial the number, then took the phone from her.

'Arbanisi Design.'

'Miss Arbanisi, please.'

'Speaking. How can I help you?'

'Miss Arbanisi, I believe you have a Miss MacLeod who works for you?'

There was silence. Beside him, the girl suddenly tried

to take the phone back. Raising his arm as a barrier, he turned his back on her, pinning her against the glass side of the box. She protested loudly, and he more or less had to shout into the mouthpiece.

'Miss MacLeod is with me. She is safe and well. Have the police been in touch with you?'

There was a little hesitation then the voice said, 'No. Not to my knowledge.'

A strange answer. Her tone was very casual. It occurred to him that they might be right there with her.

'Are they with you?' he said tentatively.

'Of course. Why don't you phone me later?'

So his hunch was correct. He chose his words carefully to make it easier for her to answer.

'We were at your home earlier this day. I'm afraid a mistake has been made. I would like to meet with you as soon as possible.'

'I see. I would have to look at my diary.'

His legs were being kicked from behind. He kicked back, though not hard. The struggling and the noise stopped.

'That might be possible.'

'I assure you, Miss Macleod has not been harmed.'

'That's excellent. I won't be at home, but you do have my mobile number, don't you?'

Once outside the box, he took the girl's arm without thinking. She whirled round, lashing out with her other hand, knocking him sideways.

'Please don't do this,' he raised his hands in defence, 'Everything will be all right, now I've spoken to her. I've told you, over and again, no one is going to hurt you. If you will just be patient for a . . .'

He moved forward but again she mistook his intentions and kicked out, missing him but sending one shiny black shoe flying into the field. Suddenly he was very weary. How much trouble could one small woman be? It was beyond comprehension.

'Are you deaf, or merely stupid? I told Miss Arbanisi, I will take full responsibility. Why can't you understand? If I'd known you would be such a nuisance, I'd have let that thug have you.'

'Don't you touch me!'

Since he'd sidestepped her and was now walking away from her, this struck him as more than a little absurd.

'Touch you? Do you see me touching you? My God, if you are the last woman on the planet I will die in flames of agony before I touch you. You don't matter. I don't want you. Do you understand? I do what I come to do and you must wait, whether you choose or not!'

Lopsided, she looked even more ridiculous than before.

'It's Irene you want,' she said.

At last. She got it at last.

'Irene's the one you want to kill.'

Losing patience, he grasped her by the arm, up-ended her until she was over his shoulder, and walked steadily back towards the house, ignoring the pummelling and screaming. The other shoe fell. He ignored that too.

At the cottage he battered the door with his heel. Laszlo unlocked it. He carried her through, remembering to duck under the wooden beam, though God knew, that might have knocked sense into her.

He dropped her onto the sofa.

'You might try feeding her, but keep your distance or she'll most likely bite you instead of the bread. I'm going back for her stupid shoes.'

Chapter Sixteen

Lazslo eyed her nervously. Clearly she'd led Feliks a bit of a dance. He wondered what had happened to the shoes. She was a pretty little thing in spite of everything. Not her fault she was caught up in all this. She was a victim of circumstance. Like himself. He'd done his best to reassure her, but what use was that, when Feliks with his sarcastic unfunny remarks was determined to do the opposite.

If things were different, if he were a tourist, meeting her somewhere by accident, they might talk over coffee and become friends. Not that coffee was always a precursor of something good. Boris had offered him Italian coffee. He'd barely taken a first sip when the great man had announced, 'I'm sending my son to Britain, and you are going with him.' He'd felt as if he'd been pushed into a lift shaft and was falling, leaving his mind disconnected and floating somewhere above him. He'd made an attempt to explain why this might not be a good idea, but his excuses were brushed aside. He was not to tell anyone where they were going or why. Specifically, he was not to tell Janek.

'But he will ask me.'

'I will tell him not to ask you,' Boris said.

Which was not as reassuring as it might have been for all sorts of reasons. Then as he turned to leave, Boris added, 'I see one of your sisters had another little girl last month.'

'Did she? I don't . . .'

'. . . keep in touch. I understand completely. You're so

busy here, and Dobruja is so far away. Congratulations anyway. Families are the backbone of our nation, Lazslo, we must all work at keeping them safe and well.'

The girl had fallen silent. Lazslo opened a brass box beside the hearth and picked out some pieces of a white compressed material with the tongs, laying them carefully on top of the small thin sticks. They burned well. The logs would come next. A good smell, the smell of burning wood. Solid and uncomplicated. He watched tiny beads of sap darken, and the flames lick along the sticks. There was no coal. Coal lasted longer but wood smelled better.

He used to like me. I used to make him laugh.

The flight had been dreadful. Feliks hadn't known who was coming with him until they met at the airport. He'd been furious. Then after the first outburst he'd hardly spoken at all, except when necessary. It was stupid to even imagine he'd want to hear Lazslo's side of things: how miserable he'd been, what little choice he'd had, all that had happened and why it had happened. They'd all depended on Feliks too much, that was the real problem. Leaderless, they'd scattered. So, whose fault was that? Not theirs, not completely. A true leader would have prepared someone else in case the worst happened. They'd believed all his big words but, behind the big words, he'd been nothing after all. Three years with those holy, sour-faced eunuchs on the mountain and he'd turned into one.

'I suppose I could eat something.'

She was looking up at him under the fringe of hair.

'Good, I will bring cake, and I will heat some soup.'

When he brought the cake to her, along with a glass of milk, she said, 'Are you Russians?'

'I think I may not tell you.'

'Because Mr Uglyface told you not to?'

'You should not call him that.'

'You don't have to pretend. I know you don't like him. Oh all right, never mind. Who were those men in Irene's flat? Do you really not know them?'

The change of subject took him by surprise.

'Not that it matters,' she went on. 'This whole thing is just one insane nightmare from start to finish. I could be at home right now watching Denzel Washington with Rachel and a tub of Haagen Dazs.'

He didn't know what she meant but she had found her voice again. That was good.

'He's making you do all this, isn't he? But you don't have to. You could let me get away now, while he's out, or later, when he's asleep.'

Or possibly it wasn't good. Not if it made Feliks angry. He shook his head, and went back to the kitchen, where tins of food stood in cardboard boxes. This at least had been properly done. The house itself was very neglected. He supposed whoever had arranged it had picked the cheapest place available without bothering to check whether it was clean or not. In a way, to do what she suggested would not be hard. Feliks trusted him with the car keys. If he wanted to, he could take the car and take her to wherever she wanted to go. If he were a different person. If his family didn't exist. If he didn't care what happened to them. He opened two tins of soup, poured them into a pot and, following the instructions on the wall carefully, powered on the gas.

Chapter Seventeen

With the girl's shoes dangling in his hand, Feliks stood in the uncut grass, watching the two figures inside the house. Lazslo had turned a light on. He was staring at the girl almost greedily, as if he'd not seen a woman for months and was ready to eat her.

There was traffic far away on the main road. Nothing closer. Before they left the city they'd lost without too much difficulty the red BMW with its dark-haired driver who might or might not have been curious about them. The sun was sinking. He tucked the shoes inside his zipped jacket and, vaulting the fence, began to go up the slope, moving from dim to darker shade and out again. The hillside was quiet, with scarcely any birdsong, though he thought he heard a noise that might be a stream somewhere. The slope grew steeper, birch giving way to closely-planted pine. He ignored the branches that caught at him, heedless of scratches.

At last he paused for breath. Beside him was a broken birch tree, shattered by wind or frost or both. Where the bark was gone, the trunk was a lustrous silver grey, and smooth, with darker, perpendicular grooves. Here and there tiny slivers protruded, like arrows broken off just below the arrowhead. A martyr tree. Some fragments of bark remained. He pulled, and off they came easily, like miniature plaster casts or the rough crusts of a wound. The trunk beneath was raw and red like a scar. A small white spider scuttled across the surface of the piece of bark in his hand.

Dimitar had been greatly upset by his face, that night when they'd talked together. He'd come via the outside window, creeping like a monkey over the sill. Feliks switched on a table lamp in the darkness. With only his hands to speak for him, the old man needed light to be heard.

'I didn't tell him where you were,' Dimitar signed.

'Did you know?'

Urgently the words took shape, 'I took you there.'

'How the hell did you . . .?' Feliks broke off, catching the agitated hands which were signing too fast for him.

'It took too long,' Dimitar told him, beginning again. 'I had to carry you to a doctor. Then three days by horse and cart to Tavcarjeva.'

'How did you get away with it? Why there?'

'Konstantin is an old friend. Boyhood. We stole apples many times together.'

He took a piece of paper from his trouser pocket and passed it over.

Feliks read aloud: 'To inform you that the new plum tree is taking root and shows signs of good health.'

'The plum tree was you,' the old man told him.

Now as he climbed on, the sound of water grew louder. He found himself on the edge of a crack in the earth. He caught hold of the nearest branch and sat down. The ground was damp. Above his head, the topmost branches on either side of the narrow crack almost touched, like the framework of a fragile roof.

'You must get away tonight,' Dimitar had told him. The Asiatic cast of the man's features had become more obvious with age, the cheekbones more pronounced, the dark eyes wearier.

'What happened to the others?'

75

'Viktor and Daniel to Romania, then to the USA. Others I don't know. Lazslo you have seen. Michal and Vanya are still locked up in the Cismigui. The charges were bogus.' The fingers made the sign for 'witnesses' and 'lying bastards'.

'But why? Why are they still there?'

'Because he couldn't hurt you.'

'What he said about the woman in Britain, is that true?'

'Yes. I think so.'

'Why does he want her? What use is she to him?'

'Don't know. Many things are changing. Many foreigners visit him. Not just the Russians. They must want something from him.'

'But he hasn't changed.' Feliks said, pulling the covers up around his chest and shoulders.

Dimitar shook his head.

'All right, I'll run, but only if you come with me. You won't get away with crossing him this time. God knows how you managed it once.'

The hands became still.

'Why do you stay with him? You've wasted nearly thirty years of your life on him, isn't that enough? Oh, I know. He rescued you from hell. But you won't save him. And it wouldn't surprise me if he believes in the fine old Hunnish tradition of slaves being buried with their masters.' He glanced at his brand new watch. 'It's almost dawn. You'd better gets back before he wakes up and sends for you.'

'You are angry with me,' the fingers signed slowly.

Was it anger, this horrible feeling? He had loved this old man all his life, and was still baffled by him.

With exaggerated slowness, the fingers moved again.

'What kind of crap question is that?' Feliks replied.

'Not crap. Tell me. Should I have let you die?'

The hands lifted his chin. The old man touched his damaged cheek, before kissing his forehead lightly. Then as silently as he had come, he was gone.

Gingerly Feliks leaned forward to see what he could of the drop. It appeared to fall away almost perpendicularly. Water rushed in a dim white line some fifteen metres below. The gap was wide enough, the ravine deep enough, the rocks at the bottom sufficiently hard. It would be easy. No more difficult than ending a spider's brief existence. He felt the cool air enter his lungs, the warmed air leave. Above him, the canopy of leaves shifted in the rising evening wind. He sat back on his heels then rose to his feet, feeling the girl's shoes shift against his chest. They were the shoes of a child who wanted to copy her older sisters, a spoiled child who shouted to get her way, and lapsed into hysterics if thwarted.

He stood up, zipped his jacket higher and began the descent. He remembered how her breasts had felt against his back when he'd carried her. And the smell of her, and her ankle bones under his hand.

Chapter Eighteen

There was no lock on the bedroom door, so Dina wedged a chair as best she could against the knob. She sat on the bed for a moment or two, then swung her legs up. The tufts of the candlewick bedspread were stiff. A faint disagreeable dust came off on her fingers. Above her, where the ceiling met the wall, thin cobwebs dangled. There was a white-painted wooden table beside the bed with dog-eared picture books and a dead clock on it, Disney pictures taped to the walls. On the wall light shade, Cinderella held hands with her Prince, infinitely adoring.

Well, she asked them, *what are my chances?*

She felt she'd been quite brave, all things considered, speaking up for herself with the nervous man. The horrible scary one had ignored her completely when he came back with her shoes, thank God. She'd never experienced real fear before, though she knew quite a lot about it. She'd written an excellent essay on 'The Fear Response', for part of her diploma. '*The thalamus takes in data from the outside world. The data is sent on to the amygdala, which in turn tells the thalamus to fight or fly.*'

Her amygdala wasn't working that well, she decided. Either evolution was a myth or she was one of the unfittest, because she still wasn't fighting or flying. She was lying on some child's bed, asking advice from a lampshade, with slow tears dribbling off her cheeks into her hair. After a while she got up, pulled the itchy bedspread down onto the carpet, and got under the duvet. It felt a bit cleaner. Images and confused bits of thoughts skittered round and round in her head. Bebe with his head hanging nearly off. The stinky smell of the phone box. The nervous one smiling, saying she wouldn't be hurt. But the other one was the boss and hadn't she seen their violence with her own eyes? They'd thought she was Irene. So had the plumbers. They crashed into Irene's furniture, over and over again, the gold and scarlet Rosedale glass goblets splintering against the wall. But what was the fight about? And did these two foreign ones want to protect Irene, or pretend to protect her so they could kidnap her? Irene was worth kidnapping. She had lots of money.

On the positive side, since the phone call Irene knew that she had been kidnapped. Irene would tell the police. And if the repair men were ok, they might give descriptions. But even if they didn't the police would be looking for her.

Without taking the duvet off completely, she shuffled out of her skirt and the ruined tights, and inspected the front of her leg. The skin wasn't broken. She hoped his bruises were worse. The nervous one wasn't so bad. He had a nice smile. He talked to her as if she was a real person.

Reaching over, she pulled on the light and took a book from the bedside table. The title was faded, silver print on a green board cover. *Secret Water* by Arthur Ransome. In childish but painstakingly neat writing on the first blank page, the original owner had inscribed his name. George C Byford 1943.

The First Lord of the Admiralty was unpopular at Pin Mill,
I hate him, said Roger, sitting on the foredeck of the Goblin with his legs dangling over the side.
'Who?' said Titty.
'The first of those lords,' said Roger.
'We all hate him,' said Titty.

She felt she was on Titty's side, although who in their right mind would call a character Titty? She attempted to read on, trying to enter a world where children had a Daddy and Mother, where they could wander unharmed in the country, with porridge for breakfast, and ginger beer and cucumber sandwiches, while her sensory cortex and hippocampus and hypothalamus raged on, sending data to and fro in her exhausted brain.

When she woke, the room was dim. Ten past three by her watch. She looked at the motionless hands of the clock, then found the key on the back and reset it. The second hand jerked its way round the face. How horribly like a spider's leg. She closed her eyes, but after a while, the discomfort low in her belly turned into proper pain. There was nothing else for it. She lifted the chair out of the way, trying to make no noise, and went out into the darker corridor. Underfoot, the lino was cold and tacky. She tugged the bathroom light cord with the very tips of her fingers, remembering how hairy and dusty it had been earlier. The light stuttered on. Gently she pushed the door shut.

Placing Kleenex around the seat, she sat as near the front as she could, trying to direct the flow forward so that it wouldn't be audible. No sooner had she finished and pulled her pants up when something huge fluttered in and out of her left ear. It darted away, and now it was flapping wildly along the light . . .

The door burst open, and he was trying to catch hold of her, demanding to know what was wrong.

She gestured upwards.

'This is all? All that screaming for this only?' He let go of her, reached towards the moth, hands cupped, and brought them together soundlessly.

'If you will raise the window, I will set him free.'

She managed it. He closed the window.

'He was probably more afraid.'

'That's so stupid. Why do people always say that? How could you possibly know?'

'Come,' he said after a moment. 'Since we are both awake, I will make some tea.'

'I don't want tea.'

He sighed. 'I have spoken again to Miss Arbanisi. We go to meet her tomorrow. You will be home soon.'

'Liar.'

He looked directly at her. 'Oh, I have many faults, Miss MacLeod, but I have never told lies. We will drink tea now, and be sensible. There has been too much stupidity.'

He switched off the light.

'I don't want tea,' she told him again.

But she did. In fact she wanted milky tea with sugar, her father's constant remedy for childhood ailments. He would prescribe antibiotics to his patients but not to his family. 'It'll either get worse or it'll get better.' She could hear him saying it. Except for eyes. Eye problems were always taken seriously.

The Arbanisi Design brochure was lying on the kitchen table. How had that got here? She supposed they must have got hold of it to find out about Irene. Rather than watch him while he made tea, she began to turn the pages, though she almost had it by heart. She'd done the proof-reading before it had gone to the printers.

Based in Glasgow, Arbanisi Design is the beloved child of Irina Arbanisi and Paul Meeten. Projects range from concept schemes through to architectural refurbishments and decoration for residential and commercial clients ... By keeping their company small, Irina and Paul ensure they are able to work closely with every client ...

Irene had drummed that into her from day one. 'Treat each client as if they were the only one. You're often the first person they speak to, Dina.' Her soft Highland accent, she learned, was a valuable asset.

Irene's photograph was on the front cover, standing over a table, with Paul sitting on the edge of it beside her, sleeves rolled up to show that he was the practical one. Neither of them was looking at the camera. She saw with surprise that her own hairstyle looked very like Irene's had four months earlier, not something she'd consciously aimed at.

Descended from European aristocracy, and a graduate in Fine Art at St Martin's, London, Irina is renowned for her innate appreciation of style and colour, while Paul, initially qualified as an architect, brings his own highly structured and disciplined approach.

She'd got the hang of the language quite quickly. 'Selective Indulgence' meant you used expensive stuff where necessary, 'authentic' was keeping some things the client already loved, or suggesting specific pieces for them to do that job. 'Experience' just meant that the same difficulty had turned up before and could be solved in the same way. 'Organic' she still wasn't sure about, but Irene said that would come with time. 'Energy' fell into the same category. It was how a room felt.

Well, this kitchen felt gross, probably not a word designers were supposed to use. Every shade of brown in the universe had been used on the walls, floor and shelves. The cups on the row of hooks would have been rejected by charity shops. The table had been upcycled with pages from The Reader's Digest Book of British Birds, glued on and coated with varnish. Not a bad idea, if it had been part of a design scheme, but it wasn't. It was just there.

'Is that a good likeness?'

'Of Irene? Yes.'

He poured tea into two cups, placing hers on the stomach of a Little Owl, who looked rather taken aback. Its black and yellow eyes stared at her, as if it expected an apology. There was milk but no sugar.

This bird is now protected by law . . . the commonest call-note is a low plaintive 'kiew-kiew' . . . She tried it out inside her head.

The curtains hadn't been closed over. He stood with his tea looking out at the night. He was wearing a black vest and the same trousers he'd had on before. Maybe he hadn't actually gone to bed. His skin was deeply tanned but there were jagged white scar lines on his shoulder and upper arm, disappearing under the vest, on the same side where his face was damaged. Whatever had happened to him must have hurt a lot, and not been dealt with quickly or expertly enough.

'It is to your liking?' he said, turning round.

She started guiltily, then realised he only meant the tea.

'Yes. Thank you.'

'You are not in this book,' he gestured to the brochure. 'Why is that?'

'Yes, I am.' She found the small photograph where her face was just visible behind Jonah's, and pushed it over so he could read the caption with all their names.

'I'm sorry. I was wrong not to believe you,' he said. 'This time tomorrow you will be rid of us. Now you must try to get some sleep.'

She didn't know where to look. Leaving the tea unfinished, she mumbled goodnight and went back to her room.

No signs of life in the world outside. No owls of any kind. No lights anywhere, except for the stars. She'd grown up in a place like this, without street light, so her ignorance of the night sky was, she knew, staggering and disgraceful. Her ignorance of so many things was staggering. She got back under the quilt and thought of her fear of moths and all small flying creatures, her father's strong hands, her childhood safe places. She wondered what the ugly man might have looked like before, and what had happened to him. His apology had flummoxed her. It wasn't fair. Her anger and dislike were being undermined, which wasn't fair. She refused to be the one who was mean and unreasonable. This soft talk was meant to fool her, keep her from causing trouble. Well, she'd cause trouble if she wanted to . . .

In all the small intervals between these flummoxing thoughts, she knew for a certainty that she'd not get back to sleep, but in this particular at least she was wrong.

Chapter Nineteen

On the day after the failed burglary, when Charles called at the Hotel where Irene Arbanisi was temporarily staying, he looked every inch the gentleman. The girl's phone had supplied him with a mobile number. He had given a name without adding any details, using the MacLeod girl's name as a reason for the request to meet. It was a great risk, but he couldn't think of a better line and in any case, what was life without the taking of risks?

When she opened the door, she was beautiful, in a different league altogether from the girl he'd mistaken for her, but just a little off balance. He suspected she hadn't slept well. She had done her best, but the pieces of her life weren't fitting together as closely as they usually did.

'What's this about? How do you know Dina?'

'Is she here?' he asked.

'No. What's this about?'

'So she hasn't been in touch with you?'

'Who are you?'

He let his face fall. 'I'm a friend of hers. I can't reach her. I thought you might know. Look, I'm sorry if this is a bad time, I'll not trouble you. Here's my card – ' he reached into his inside pocket, and selected one which identified him as an actuary for a reputable international firm. 'You could let me know . . .' he let his voice trail off in barely-controlled disappointment.

'You'd better come in, I suppose,' she said.

And this was all that it took. Time after time, this was all that it took. A well-made suit, a modicum of aftershave, a gentle voice and a business card. Thank God for the natural goodness and gullibility of humankind.

Following her through into the small sitting area, he caught sight of himself in a narrow mirror, and raised one fair eyebrow, as if to ask, what *are* you doing here, Charlie boy? He was not altogether sure, to tell the truth. He was a little tired, a little sore and stiff.

'All right, I'm listening,' she said, not inviting him to sit.

'There was a break-in at your flat yesterday.'

'Indeed there was. How do you know? And how did you get my mobile number?'

'Dina called me. That was about all she said before she was cut off.'

He was winging it now, which was what he liked best, watching her face for the slightest change, the most minute signal which would tell him what he needed to know.

'She's really not here?'

'No. I told you.'

'Then where is she? Are the police looking for her?'

'I believe so. Why ask me? You should be asking them. How do you know Dina?'

Good, you're getting there now. All the questions you should have asked before you let me in.

He assumed a troubled expression, 'I don't trust them. I suppose I thought she might have tried to get in touch with you. She looks up to you so much. She gave me your mobile number once in case . . .' He lowered his head again.

Come on, lady, I want to find the bastard who kicked me in the balls and made it necessary for me to tidy up all these loose ends, something I hadn't planned on doing. And right now you are the lady of the moment, because either you know them, or your secretary does, and one way or another, you are going tell me who and where they are.

Irene studied the top of his lowered head. She was very tired, not having slept at all well in the hotel bed. She'd been deeply upset by the news of Bebe's death, more angry than sad. Her home had been violated, her beloved cat killed, her property stolen, her work schedule put on hold and, to crown it all, the police had more or less accused her of being incompetent.

There's been an incident.

They'd watched her, heartless, cold as dead fish, not letting Paul or anyone else stay to comfort her, talking to her as if it was all her fault, all those valuables, a safe but no alarm system, hardly any security, as if she'd deliberately sent Dina into danger, as if she should have known her flat was about to be burgled. Dina seemed to be the centre of everyone's concern. Had she run off? Could she have known the thief? She'd called 999, but that proved nothing. If she wasn't involved, where might she have gone? The same questions, over and over. And no, no, you can't go home, not yet, we'll find you a hotel, we're so very sorry.

They were still there when the phone rang. Anger had given her power. Instantly, in the twinkling of an eye, she'd managed to gain back her self-control. The word 'Irina' had done it. A male voice, but no one called her that except her mother. She'd swung the chair round, so the two police officers couldn't see her face. She'd fooled them completely. She knew more than they did now. And now here was another stranger preoccupied with Dina. He'd called before she was properly awake, asking if he might to speak to her, and claiming to be a friend of Dina's. Did he mean 'boyfriend'? Was this Derek's replacement? That was

87

hard to believe. Dina was merely nice looking, but he was almost too good to be true. Six feet tall, well put together, unruly blond curls. She wondered fleetingly about body hair. She had always preferred smooth men.

'You look pale, Miss Arbanisi,' he said. 'I shouldn't have come.'

'I haven't slept," she said.

'I know the feeling,' he said, with a woebegone smile.

'I'm sorry, please sit down,' she said.

He took the other tub chair. His socks perfectly matched the dark grey of his pinstripe suit. His brogues marked him as a traditional man, but the bright tie suggested otherwise.

'They don't know what's happened to Dina,' she told him.

'They?'

'The police. They came to my office. They think a man was burgling my flat, but then Dina came in, and they think he attacked her and she managed to stab him and call for help, but then she ran away before the police got there.'

She watched carefully to see his reaction.

'She stabbed someone? Dina stabbed someone? I can't believe it.' The blue eyes fixed on her, imploring her to make it not true.

'He died. He bled to death apparently.'

His mouth froze, mouth open in horrified disbelief.

'I know. It's impossible. That's what I told them. Dina's a dizzy little butterfly of a thing. She spends her every waking moment helping people. She flits and flutters, she couldn't hurt anyone. She'd never touch a knife. She'd faint if she saw one.'

He was holding his hands to his head. She hesitated. Was she being unfair? Should she put him out of his misery and tell him the truth? Or should she twist the knife a little more and mention the other idiotic police theory that

Dina might have been part of the crime from the start. Perhaps he was suffering enough.

'They're just being horrible. They won't let me go home because it's a crime scene.'

'I know how lovely your place is. Dina's told me about it. We were supposed to go out for a meal last night, you see,' he added.

She felt a flush of jealousy. How on earth had Dina attracted a man like this? Where had they met? Why had she said nothing about it? It wasn't like Dina to keep anything secret.

'There's only one problem . . .'

He looked up questioningly.

'Some of my property is missing. So there might have been someone else there. Unless Dina took it.'

He looked so miserable, she felt almost like slapping him. All this for Dina.

'I should have asked, did he do much damage? To your house? I've never been burgled, so I won't lie and say I understand, but I do realise this must be dreadful for you.'

His eyes were so blue. Could he be wearing contact lenses?

'The worst thing really was, my cat was killed.'

'Why? Oh, this is awful. This just gets worse and worse.' He moved to the couch where she was sitting, though not too close. He took her hand and gave it a brief squeeze. Then he made a face, as if feeling that he overstepped himself, and went back to his chair.

'Well, in fact, I know one or two things that the police don't,' she found herself saying. 'Things I haven't told them.'

She had his full attention.

'I got a phone call last night,' she said. 'Well, two actually, there was one before that.' She stopped. How would he react? What would he think of her? She didn't want him to think badly of her. Not when she hardly knew him.

'It was a foreign man. At least, he sounded foreign. He said his name, but I don't remember it. He said that he'd come to see me, got into the fight by accident and the knifing wasn't deliberate, and he had Dina with him. He wants me to come and get her.'

He digested this slowly, saying finally, 'What did you tell him?'

'Well, I didn't know what to say. I told him I'd think about it. He wouldn't let me talk to her, but he said she was fine, not hurt at all, that it's all been a misunderstanding. Of course, it could all be a pack of lies. I haven't told the police yet. I suppose I ought to.'

The blond man raised his eyes to the ceiling, as if he was thanking God, then lay back in his chair, both hands over his face. She noted how his shoulders shook ever so very slightly with relief.

Chapter Twenty

The village street was busy, but Lazslo saw a space and pulled in.

'It's a double yellow line,' the girl objected. 'You can't stop here.'

'It's fine. This will do,' Feliks said.

'You'll get a ticket. A small place like this is a traffic warden's dream come true.'

'I think she is right.' Lazslo said.

'Then we will drive on. We have no need to stop.'

'Excuse me. I was told at breakfast that I could shop for whatever I needed. I can't meet Irene looking like this. Not if you want to convince her you've been nice to me.'

She had a point, he thought. It was exactly what he'd said, but she reminded him of those small petulant dogs with more hair than brains. And sharp little teeth. He'd liked her better during the night when she was terrified. Perhaps he needed a supply of moths.

'Very well. But you speak to no one. Lazslo will go with you.'

They parked eventually in a side street some distance from the shops. 'Tell me, what is it you do for Miss Arbanisi?' he heard Lazslo ask as they walked away together. Lazslo was beginning to irritate him again. When the girl objected to his smoking in the car, he'd at once rolled down the window and flipped his cigarette into the road. When she thanked him, he'd smiled like a cat being tickled under its chin.

He studied what was visible of the main street in the mirror. Well-fed middle-aged women in trousers. Always in trousers, as if skirts were against the law. A young father with a child on his shoulders. Old men in heavy wool jackets, despite the warmth of the sun. A very large orange tractor trundled slowly and noisily past, with a queue of cars behind it. There was no way of knowing whether their car was known to the police, but most likely their descriptions were by now. The wounded man and his friend would have said all they could, to vindicate themselves if for no other reason. According to the girl, they were workmen who'd come to fix something. She had only screamed because the cat was dead. If so, the whole thing was a farce. He and Lazslo had intervened quite unnecessarily. But workmen with knives? That seemed unlikely.

What was taking them so long? He watched a pigeon attack a piece of cardboard on the pavement. It had more wisdom than he did. At least it stopped when it saw how pointless its actions were.

Well, what was done was done. The mistake was his, it had been his decision to go in. If it had been a decision at all. And he would pay for it. But for now, what else was there to do but go forward? All he asked for now was the chance to speak to the Arbanisi woman. Once the message was conveyed, he would let the police find him. In fact, he might find them first.

He was here in this strange country by his own choice; he had agreed to come because his father had agreed to his terms. Which he might or might not fulfil. Lazslo had been a sly and dirty trick on his father's part. He was useful, of course, and not merely as a driver. Despite his limited language skills, his perfect memory retained everything: their base, this new meeting place and all the route details. Then he wondered if Lazslo had been Janek's idea. It fitted his twisted sense of humour. Janek was arguably the crueller of the two. Boris had been less inclined to indulge in sadism. In the past.

But who could be sure? He smiled grimly. The past had much to answer for. Like this driving business. One more fault on his part. He would never be able to drive a car again. Lazslo had left the keys in the ignition, knowing there was no chance that Feliks would take the driver's seat.

At last they reappeared. Lazslo, in his new role as slave and pet cat, was bearing two large white plastic bags. The girl's face was flushed for some reason. Was she angry? Maybe he hadn't given Lazslo enough cash. He didn't look all that cheerful either. Once in the back seat, she pulled a lipstick out of the bag and began applying the bright paste to her lips. Then she began brushing her hair.

'Shall we move on? If you're not too busy watching the show,' he said to Lazslo, in their own tongue.

They arrived at the ancient castle well ahead of the appointed time. The approach road was narrow, with high grassy banks on both sides. Beyond the open entrance gate there was a wide grey-gravelled parking area. Two cars sat there already, basking in the late morning sunshine. Both Volvos, one red, one silver. German number plates.

'Do you recognise those cars?' Feliks asked her.

'No,' she said. She had tidied herself up reasonably well, he thought, viewing her in the mirror. She would never be a beauty, but she looked all right. She was wearing a different blouse. When had that happened? Blue material with stripes, like a man's shirt. It made her look sensible.

'Wait here, please,' he told her, motioning to Lazslo to get out.

It was a good choice of meeting place. Public, but not at all crowded, with good visibility all round. The courtyard surrounded the two towers of the ancient sandstone building. Tall beech trees in bright leaf, just beginning to turn, pines much like those at home, other smaller trees he didn't recognise. Three picnic benches, well-tended flower beds full of red and yellow roses. Their sweet perfume was just perceptible. Over to their left, a small green shack bore the universal signs for male and female, one at either end. There was another shack with a 'Private' sign and a padlock. A flagstone path led to the doorway of the tower.

'How much did you spend on her?' he asked.

'Not so much. She said she needed clean things to wear. And new shoes. 'Keep her happy' was what you said. 'We have to keep her happy."

She didn't look happy, watching them keenly through the closed window. He tried a smile. She looked away.

'What do we do now?' Lazslo asked. He'd lit a cigarette and with his free hand was flicking his index fingernail back and forth against his thumbnail, making tiny clicking sounds. Feliks felt a sudden pang. The intervening years vanished. It was the old Lazslo, wanting to be helpful, nervous as hell, waiting for the roof to fall on them.

'We're supposed to meet inside. I'll take her in. You wait here,' he said. All at once he wanted Lazslo out of his sight.

'Shouldn't we stay together? What if Miss Arbanisi's already inside?'

'I don't think she is. The cars mean nothing to the girl. And we're early. Relax. It's going to be ok. When Miss Arbanisi comes, the girl will come out and wait with you. But you don't even need to speak to her.'

'What if the police come with her? I'd rather we stayed together. I don't feel . . .'

'No, you're the lookout. You were always my lookout man, ok?'

He held out his hand. Lazslo clasped it in the old way.

'What's wrong?' Apart from his own so very smooth hypocrisy . . .

Lazslo was looking back toward the entrance, shading his eyes against the sun. 'That lane's too narrow. I was sure there was another one. I'm positive there was on the map. I've a bad feeling about this.'

'Relax. We're only the messengers, right? Twenty-four hours from now we'll be on the plane home.'

How impressive and sincere he sounded. Lazslo fell for it, managed a faint smile as he pushed his hair out of his eyes. His tongue showed between his lips. Another old familiar sign of anxiety. Would it all happen so easily? The British police were not fools. Miss Arbanisi might indeed be bringing them with her, despite her promises not to.

'Come on, pretend you're a tourist. Go sit at one of those benches and have a smoke. Count the hairs on the sparrows.'

It was a joke from the old days, advice given by anyone to anyone else who was worried about anything, a confusion of bible verses about sparrows being valuable and the hairs on one's head being numbered. Lazslo remembered, and smiled again.

His own smile fading, Feliks watched him walk away towards the trees. *What happened to you?* he wondered. *Damn Janek to hell for whatever he did to you.*

Despite his instructions, the girl had got out of the car. She was looking up at the ancient towers. There was a low parapet around the top of the nearest one, at least sixty feet above the ground. No guard rail.

'Come, we'll go inside,' he said. 'Lazslo is going to sit in the sun and have a quiet smoke till Miss Arbanisi arrives. Perhaps you could smile,' he added. 'The woman at the door is looking at us with great curiosity.'

'Why do we have to go in?'

He was so tempted to say, in a deep, menacing voice,

'So that I may lure you to your death, and Miss Arbanisi also.' But really, she had been through enough, and none of it her fault. In her world, so completely unlike Janek's, moral choices still existed, with moral consequences. Quite possibly she had never even questioned this.

'I am going to make her very rich and happy,' he said. It was still possible. And the police might not come. Anything was possible.

The custodian was a buxom woman with white hair struggling to free itself from a chignon. She told them they were just in time for the next tour, so they followed her broad rear up a narrow winding stair into a large empty room with high, mesh-covered windows. A group was waiting for them. Two men, two women, three bored-looking teenagers. One of the men was filming the wooden beams of the ceiling.

The guide began her talk. Feliks watched the girl beside him. She was looking intently at the other people. Was she thinking of speaking to them?

'Miss MacLeod. Dina,' he said softly, 'please trust me for one more hour. This is nearly over for you. All will be well.'

'You wouldn't let me go yesterday in case I told the police about you. What's different now?'

'When I have spoken to Miss Arbanisi, what happens to me is not so important. I have to give her something.'

The guide was still talking, and the others followed her over to the far wall to examine something of interest.

'So I can go straight to the police and tell them everything?'

'If you want to. If you waited for just a few hours, that would be kind. You might consider that we did believe those men were hurting you, and that Lazslo wounded his assailant in self-defence.'

Like a coiled toy from a box, the questions shot out

again. Workmen? If not, who were they? Sent by whom? No one was supposed to know why he and Lazslo were here. Boris trusted no one, wanted no records, nothing written or taped. Nobody was meant to know.

Leave it he told himself. There was no time now for this. All depended on the next half hour. All the Arbanisi woman had to do was make one phone call to the number he would give her. She would surely do that. She had nothing to lose. One simple message would then wing its way to Boris.

He stared at an immense cobweb on the dusty stone window ledge. *Am I the fly? Who is the spider?*

The guide and her followers were disappearing through a low doorway in the far corner of the room. He looked at the world outside. Long-legged sheep with blue paint on their rumps were feeding on lush grass. Small birds sat on the electricity wires. On the main road, a white car slowly turned into the lane.

He crossed to the window at the other side of the room. There was a red BMW beside the other cars. He couldn't see if there was anyone inside. Nor could he see Lazslo.

'I suppose you have diplomatic immunity,' the girl said.

Did he? He wasn't at all sure. He wasn't sure of anything. Should he go out? Stay put? She turned away, as if to follow the tourists. He caught her by the wrist.

'Let go of me.'

'No, stay with me. Your friend is here, I think. A white Lexus, right?'

'Irene?' Her face suffused with relief.

'We will go down now to meet her. Once you confirm to me that it is her, you do whatever you wish.'

They waited in the small entrance way for a few minutes. At last there came the sound of a woman's high heels clicking on the flagstones.

'Irene! Oh, thank God!'

The woman opened her arms to meet the hurtling figure. Feliks felt tension drain from him like grain from a sack. This was surely the real thing. Beautifully dressed, with a slender figure, hair the colour of first wheat. He let the embrace and the conversation go on for a time, delighted to hear Dina confirm what he'd told this woman, that he was no burglar, that he was in fact some kind of rescuer, but when she began to elaborate on events he interrupted.

'Miss Arbanisi, as I said last night, my name is Feliks Albescu. First I'm instructed to give you something to establish that what I say is trustworthy.'

He took a small brown leather box out of his pocket.

'What's this?

'Please.'

The woman stared at its contents.

'How did you get this?'

'You recognise it?'

'Of course.' She slipped the ring onto her finger. The huge emerald seemed to flash fire even in the dim light inside the entrance room. Her fingernails, he noted, were beautifully manicured.

'Is that real?'

'If it's what I think it is,' she held out her hand for Dina to see. 'How did you get this? Where did it come from?' she asked him.

'Miss Arbanisi, I am here to offer you your proper inheritance. There is much at home that is rightfully yours if you are willing to claim it.'

It sounded like something memorised, which it exactly was.

'My inheritance?'

He went on with his script, 'Miss Arbanisi, you will be aware that our country has almost four years ago rejected

Communism. The president and people now wish to offer your family those titles and lands which your great-grandfather was forced to renounce. The Archduchess Annamaria's ring is a token of goodwill. You are to keep it, whatever you . . .'

He broke off.

'Hey, what're you . . .' the girl protested as he pushed her behind him.

Miss Arbanisi turned to address the approaching figure, 'Charles, I was right. Look at this! He *is* from the Old Country . . .'

'Stop there!' Feliks raised one hand, kept the other behind him to keep the girl back.

'Oh, this is a friend of Dina's,' Miss Arbanisi said.

'Look here, old boy, calm down. I'm harmless,' the man said at the same time, taking a step backwards.

Feliks looked from one to the other.

'What?' the girl was squeaking behind him.

'This man is your *friend*?' he turned to her.

'Irene, what on earth are you . . .?'

'But this is the man who attacked you.'

'Well, not exactly,' she began, 'You sort of attacked him.'

She was crazy. They were all crazy. He needed Lazslo to back him up. 'Lazslo!' he shouted. Again, louder. Nothing.

'You. Whoever you are.' He faced the blond man, 'Tell Miss Arbanisi what happened yesterday. Tell her.'

The man smiled, as if the whole situation simply amused him.

'Oh, I don't think that's necessary, do you? People might get hurt. You don't want that.'

The world shifted, as smoothly as a piece of music changing key. It was the look in the fellow's eyes, not the words, not even the tone of his voice. It seemed to Feliks that he had met this man not once before but many times.

In a uniform or plain clothes, on the side of the power-ful, against the side of righteousness, he was the man who didn't care. The man who always had the last word, who would sleep soundly at night no matter what he had done. Reading Shakespeare, in his student days, Feliks had con-sidered the playwright mistaken. In his experience, it was quite possible to read the heart in the face.

'Irene, would you and Dina wait for us in the garden? Feliks and I need to have a little talk,' the man said.

Irene looked up from her hand. 'Oh Charles, don't be silly. Dina's fine. She's not hurt at all. He came to meet me, and I want to talk to him now.'

'We can talk later, Miss Arbanisi,' Feliks said. 'Please do as he asks.'

He studied the man's clothing for a bulge, saw none. There might be a gun, nevertheless. Dina was staring at him. 'Go,' he implored her silently. 'Don't argue. Do what I say. Go.'

He saw she was baffled, hesitant, as if waiting for the older woman to tell her what to do. He shaped the word, 'Please', begging her to trust him without a reason, to be sensible for once, to recognise that something important was happening.

'Irene, let's go. Let them have their talk,' she said.

Outnumbered, Miss Arbanisi went reluctantly out with her into the sunlight.

'You're not actually a friend of hers?' Feliks said.

'Of course not.'

He was relieved. But who was he then, and where the hell was Lazslo?

'Who are you working for?' he asked.

'Who do you think?' the blond man smiled again.

Clearly a man who liked to show off his fine white teeth.

100

American? The Americans were famous for their fine dentistry. He sounded English. He could be anything. He could be the devil incarnate.

'There are people above,' Feliks said. 'If we remain here, they may easily descend and interrupt us.'

'Oh well, we can't have that, can we? We'd better find ourselves a nice private corner.'

Chapter Twenty-One

Dina looked round the courtyard. One car that hadn't been there before. The driver was leaning against the boot, talking on his phone, paying no attention to them at all.

'Irene? Who *is* that? He told me he was fixing the washing machine. How do you know him?'

Irene was holding the ring up to the light. It sparkled magnificently.

'Irene, who *is* he?'

'Who?'

'And why on earth did you say he was a friend of mine?'

'Well, I didn't know it was meant to be a secret. He was very worried about you. I think this *is* genuine. It's much bigger in real life than it looks in the painting. It's almost indecent.'

'What painting?'

'You know, sweetie, you might have mentioned him before now. Where did you find him?'

'I didn't. He was in the flat when . . .'

'Don't worry, I'm not jealous. He's very concerned about you, you lucky girl. I suspect he's giving that horrid man a real talking-to. I just hope that's all he does.'

'Irene,' Dina began, through gritted teeth, repressing the desire to scream, 'You're not listening. I've only seen him once in my life. And it was a real fight, Irene, the other man got stabbed – '

'Oh, don't flap, Dina. The police told me about it. I

know it was an accident. He told me all about it on the phone last night. But he didn't mention this.'

The ring, the whole ring, nothing but the bloody ring! She wanted to snatch it off Irene's hand. Which he? What phone call? It was too much. The sun was in her face, high and blinding.

'I know, it's very beautiful, Irene, but something's wrong. Something's really wrong here. I think we . . . could we just get in your car and – '

'Don't paw at me, Dina. You don't understand. I've dreamed all my life about going back. My father died talking about it. Now it's all starting to come true.' She held up her hand. 'Look at it, sweetie. It's the Sisi Emerald. It was a gift from the young Empress Elizabeth to the Archduchess. It's absolutely priceless.' Her eyes narrowed as she looked back at the tower. 'This is ridiculous. I know he was upset, especially at the idea that you might have been involved in the burglary, but they should have finished their little squabble by now.'

Dina watched Irene check the back of her hair, then step carefully across the grass towards the entrance door. Involved? What was she talking about? Not one word of apology, or sympathy, or concern. She didn't know whether to weep, laugh, scream or all three.

Something glinted in the grass beneath her feet. Car keys. Bending down she recognised the tag. These keys belonged to Lazlso's car. She looked around. It was still where it had been. Irene had parked the Lexus at the far side where there was some shade under the beech trees. No sign of Lazslo.

The car was less than twenty feet away. She had the keys. She didn't have to stay a minute longer, didn't have to be here in the middle of all this insanity. It was nothing to do with her any more. Hadn't the ugly one said so himself? Why should she care what happened to him?

'Why is he so rude all the time?' she'd asked Lazslo. They were in the queue in the chemist's, and Lazslo was looking at his watch,

'He hates everyone,' Lazslo had answered. 'Women especially.'

'Why?'

'A woman ruined his life.'

He paid for her purchases and they went outside. She asked to go into another shop to buy underwear and a new blouse. He stood beside her as she searched the rails, trying to make suggestions as to what she might like.

'What did she do to him, this woman?' she asked, trying to sound casual.

'Nothing. She died because of him. He knew it was his fault. So then he got drunk, always the big drinker, you know? But this time he crashed the car. He was broken everywhere,' Lazslo gestured up and down his own body. 'The face, you see that yourself. We thought he was dead, but in fact he ran away. In fact, he's a complete kastrat.'

'A what?'

His face went pink.

'I mean, he went to be a priest.'

She didn't think that was what the word meant. But maybe it didn't mean what she thought it meant. She stared at the display of silver bangles and rings in a locked glass cabinet. When the bangles lost their excitement, she turned her attention to the shoes next to them. Expensive brands and not her style, but there were some sandals, reduced. She grasped the first pair of size fours, tried them and held them up for approval. He made no objection. Again he paid for everything, in cash.

But even if that part of his story was true . . . he might be wrong about the hatred thing. He'd been all right when they were drinking tea during the night. He had stepped in front of her, when the blond man arrived, as if he wanted to protect her. And such intensity when he'd pleaded silently to her to leave. None of that felt like hatred.

Not that she cared what happened to any of them, but just thinking objectively, she decided, it probably wasn't as simple as Lazslo thought It was more like self-hatred, with a lot of misery mixed in. She'd seen some of her father's patients react that way – farm workers with injuries from machinery, or lobster fishermen out on their own who'd been careless in bad weather. In Aberdeen she'd nursed one young man who'd hurt himself badly, lost all his left-hand fingers on a rig in Angola. Of course it turned out he'd been left-handed. He'd cursed all day, but he'd been seen crying in the night.

The two German families were coming out of the tower. Down at the end of the lane, more cars were arriving. A woman driving the first one, with a man on the passenger side. And behind it, unmistakeably, a police car.

Walking, running, Dina reached and crossed the entrance room, saw no one on the first floor and ran up the first spiral staircase, only to be blocked by Irene.

'Oh Dina, get out of the way . . .'

'The police are here!'

'The police? How the hell did they . . .? Oh, do move over, Dina!'

She pushed past.

Dina leaned against the wall for a moment or two, recognised that she had no clue why she was doing this, decided to go on, and climbed up the next short flight. There was no one on the second floor either. Was there another way out? The next set of stairs was narrower and longer. She ducked through a low doorway, finding herself on the parapet.

The wall was waist high. No handrail. She edged cautiously round the corner.

Feliks and the other man were fighting, locked together. 'The police are here!' she yelled. 'Stop it!'

But they *had* heard, for the knot untangled, and they fell apart. Flushed, dishevelled, Feliks turned.

'They're here! The police!' she shouted at him.

He didn't seem to understand. But the fair-haired man did. He ducked, swung at Feliks and pushed past towards her. Feliks lunged, trying to pull him back.

Move, her brain said, but there was nowhere to go. Whirl, rush, tumbling, and something hard smacking the breath out of her, she was off her feet, sliding down something rigid and hot, pain in the back of her head, scrabbling for something to hold. At last her shoes caught, held against something . . .

. . . she heard whimpering, the sounds of a small, hurt animal. Then she understood that she was the one making the sounds, that she was on her back on a steep tile roof, that the blueness filling her eyes was sky, that if she moved the slightest fraction she was going to come apart and be concertina'd into a heap of bones on the gravel below.

Chapter Twenty-Two

Someone was talking somewhere. The world beyond her tightly-shut eyes was bright with shining points of light, then went darker. There was a weight on top of her, over her face. She couldn't breathe. It shifted. She screamed, or tried to. No sound emerged from her mouth. More weight, across her middle. Then a voice right in her ear, telling her to be still. When she opened her eyes, Feliks's face was inches from her. She could smell his sweat. His beard was touching her forehead.

'I have you. Don't move.'

He said it again. A strange high, mewing noise came out of her.

'Put your arm around my neck. All the way round.'

She couldn't. Her arms were rigid at her sides, fingers pasted to the burning roof tiles.

'Listen to me. I have a secure place. I'm not going to fall. If you hold onto me, you will be all right. Do it now.'

She found his neck, embedded her fingers in it.

'Now, the other hand.'

'No.'

'Yes. You can do this.'

But she couldn't. Not till his hand was on hers, prising it off like a starfish, finger by finger, then placing it over his shoulder to meet and clutch the first hand. At least the high whimpering sound had stopped . . .

Now they were moving slowly, her body beneath his, the

tiles scraping her back, and the back of her head, but they were moving, sideways, and all the time he was talking, telling her all was well, she was safe, all would be well . . .

When she could open her eyes, she was standing upright facing a stone wall. Light all around her. So she was outside. He was behind her, supporting her, his arms locked around her. They were, she realised, on the second tower, separated from its twin by about twenty feet of steeply sloping roof. She had evidently fallen on this. Somehow he had reached her and covered her, moved the two of them sideways to safety. If she had fallen more to the right . . .

'Miss MacLeod!'

She looked towards the voice.

'Stay where you are, please.'

It was a man she didn't recognise, standing across from them on the ledge of the upper tower.

'She is not hurt!' Feliks called to him. 'I'll bring her down.'

He more or less carried her across a landing to a stairwell. They stood for a while, then she managed a few steps down, with him going backwards, holding her by both arms.

'You can't,' she said. 'You can't go down. I think he's a policeman.'

'Yes, I believe so. It's all right.'

'But you can't let them get you.'

'Unless we can quickly grow wings, I think we have not much choice.'

'But what . . . what am I going to say to them?'

'Whatever pleases you. The truth.'

Her left foot went sideways. He steadied her.

'Whatever they ask you, you must tell them,' he said, guiding her onto the next step, and the next. 'There's one thing I'm curious about. Who is that man, whose eyes are bluer even than Lazslo? Why was he there with you?'

She stopped. 'He was in Irene's flat when I got there. I don't know him. And I don't think Irene knows him either.'

The sound of voices rumbled up from below. From here on down the steps became wider. There was a metal handrail. Feliks kept her other hand, turning to face the way down, finally letting her go. She hesitated for a few moments, pushing her hair behind her ears, trying to dust her brand new shirt front, trying to straighten her skirt, but it hurt her hands too much.

The entrance hall was full of people. Feliks was being talked to by the man who had shouted at them. There were men in police uniform, and a stout woman in plain clothes, and the custodian and another policeman trying to get a couple of ordinary people not to come in. *I need to sit down*, Dina told herself. *I need to lie down, really.* Abruptly there was the stout woman holding her by the arm, saying her name. Out of the blur, someone offered her water in a bottle, which she drank greedily. They were all being ushered out into the courtyard. She tried to see where Feliks was, but the detective woman held onto her, which was annoying. The water was so beautiful. She'd forgotten cold water could taste so good. She could see it running down her throat like a long silver line . . .

'Can I sit down, please,' she said.

'Just a moment.'

'I need to sit down.'

Her legs felt like jelly. So ignoring them all, she sat down on the grass. She put her head between her knees as they'd been taught to. It helped a little.

'Where's the Arbanisi woman?' the stout woman asked, bending down to her. 'Where is she? Is she inside?'

Dina raised her head. The custodian lady was standing on the path, talking to a dark-haired man in a navy sweater.

109

They were both watching her. And there was Feliks, not so far away.

'I don't know,' she said.

Feliks called to her, 'Have you seen Lazslo?'

'He wasn't here when I came out with Irene.'

'What's that?' the woman asked sharply. 'Was she here? Who is this Lazslo?'

'Something is wrong,' Feliks called again. 'He wouldn't leave without me. And the car is still there.'

He was right. Dina's hand went to her skirt and felt the keys. She looked round for the blond man, but he was missing too. And no Irene. What was happening? Had aliens beamed everyone up?

The male detective barked instructions at the uniformed officers, who scattered. He took over from the woman. He steered Dina by the elbow a little further away from Feliks and the policeman beside him. He drew her to her feet. His fingers were hard, like steel pincers, right on the places that were already sore . . .

'What are you doing?'

'Calm down. Nobody's going anywhere . . .'

Which was, she thought, a ridiculous thing to say, since everybody had already disappeared off the face of the earth . . .

'This is going to be a lot easier if you just relax. You don't need to talk to that guy over there, he's doing his own thing, he's not in any trouble. I'm the one here with you. Anything you want to talk about, talk to me.'

She didn't want to talk to him at all, with his bony fingers and bad breath. She wanted Feliks. He looked so miserable. All she could think was that Lazslo and Irene and the man called Charles had all gone off together, had abandoned him, abandoned them both, Irene with her head full of the stupid emerald, and Charles because he knew he was in

110

trouble, and Lazslo because . . . oh, because he'd just had enough. It wasn't fair. Everyone could run away except her . . .

'Are you arresting him? He hasn't done anything. It was that other man . . .'

'Of course it was. No, stay with me, petal. No one's being arrested. We'd just like to clear up some stuff. You're in quite a lot of bother, you know. There's a man dead, and we know you were there. You need to answer a few questions for me.'

Later she wondered if it was the word 'petal' that did it, more than fear, mention of a dead man, or the shock of being accused, or the smell of him and the pain in her elbows. She pulled herself free and was running before he could stop her. She keyed the doors and jumped into the car. Suddenly Feliks was falling in at the other side, trying to wrestle the key from her hand, but already it was in the ignition, and the engine roared into life. Someone thumped on the bonnet. She jammed the car into reverse, then catapulted forward, too close to the wire mesh fence on one side, doing dreadful grinding damage to the paint-work, and the engine roaring, revving in too high a gear, out into the approach road, and Feliks clinging to the inside roof and the seat, his door open. At the main road, without even looking, she swung left, changed gear and floored the accelerator. The passenger door fell shut as she swerved. From somewhere behind them came a squeal of brakes and a loud bang, but she didn't look back.

Chapter Twenty-Three

'Stop the car,' Feliks yelled, above the engine roar and the sound of car horns beside and behind, and the persistent dinging sound that told them no one was wearing belts.

'No.'

'We have to. This is pointless.'

'I don't care.'

But to his relief she lessened speed.

He looked back. 'They don't follow us. At least we should talk. Please.'

At last she eased her foot from the accelerator, enough to turn off into what looked like a disused depot of some kind. Red brick buildings with broken windows, long purple weeds sprouting from the roofs, thin grasses growing through cracks in the concrete. Corrugated fencing. No sign of life.

'Drive over there behind those buildings,' he told her.

When they stopped, he got out, walked a few paces away from the car, and sat down against a wooden fence. His heart was still thumping. His neck was sore where her nails had dug into it, and his body was now telling him in how many places the blond man's fists had landed successfully. Nowhere to hide here, when the police came.

Try, though. Walk away.

Sure. I'll do that. Once I start breathing normally.

Let her do the explaining. Let them question her.

It wouldn't go that way. He saw himself, as in a line of

reflecting mirrors, being quizzed by a succession of face-less men, his own face growing smaller and fainter in the distance until he dwindled into nothing. He would be lost. His friends, for whose sake alone he had agreed to do this, would be lost. It would all have been for nothing.

What had possessed her? She could have killed them both. She was staring straight ahead through the wind-screen. Her face was ghostly pale, streaked where tears had run through the dusty marks. He saw her fall again, felt the shock, and the heat of her body beneath him, the terror in her eyes, and how tightly she'd clung to him once they began to move towards the ledge and safety.

He got up and walked slowly back to the car.

He opened the driver's door. 'What possessed you?'

She didn't answer.

'You could have killed us both. You are crazy,' he told her.

'And you're normal.'

He dropped his head on to his arm on the door frame, forcing himself not to swear.

'All you had to do was tell them what happened. Did you think I would deny it?'

Still she stared into space.

He didn't understand. She had done nothing wrong. Why didn't she want to talk to the police?

There was a half-full bottle of water at her feet. He reached in for it and drank till it was almost gone, pouring the last inch over his head and face. He flung it at the fence, startling a bird perched high and safe on the telegraph wire. Still no sign of police cars on the main road. Why had she wanted to run? Was it possible that she'd lied to him, that she did know the man in the suit? What *had* been going on in Miss Arbanisi's house?

He tried again. 'I will not tell them what you were doing.

That's your business. Although perhaps you would be best to tell her yourself, even if your friend isn't pleased.' And who was he to judge in any case?

She looked up at him.

'I don't have to know, Miss MacLeod. I'm not interested in what games you three were playing, why you were screaming . . .'

'I screamed because of Bebe.'

'Who is Bebe?'

'Irene's cat. I stood on him.' She put her hands over her face. 'I don't know why. He said a man was killed. I can't do this anymore.'

She was sobbing properly, her shoulders heaving.

His brain felt as if it had been dropped, dismantled and badly put back together. Who'd been killed? The one with the knife wound? Who was this blond man if he wasn't known to either woman? What did he want with Miss Arbanisi? An intense weariness spread through him, as if the earth's gravity had suddenly trebled. He dropped back into the passenger seat.

'If you don't believe me, ask Irene,' she said, in a whisper.

It was an excellent plan, if he'd known where Irene was. But he didn't. In time, the police would find her too. He would tell the police as much as he could, and let them do the rest.

They sat in silence for a long time. Beyond the rim of the yard, large birds, crows perhaps, were circling brokenly above a huddle of trees, wheeling and falling like torn pieces of black paper above a bonfire. And still the police didn't come.

She spoke first. 'Was it true, all that stuff you told Irene? The ring and everything?'

He nodded. Did they shoot crows to avert bad luck in this country?

'So you're really here from your government?'

It was an excellent question. Strange that he'd not thought of it in those terms at all.

'So you can go to your Embassy. They'll talk to the police for you and . . .'

'It's not that easy.'

'But it would be. That's what Embassies are for. My friend Sophie lost her passport in Turkey and they were really nice to her, even though she'd just lost it, not had it stolen and they . . .'

How very simple her world was.

'You don't understand.'

'I understand enough. I understand you'd rather faff around like a headless chicken feeling miserable than actually do something.'

Chapter Twenty-Four

'What exactly are we doing?' Irene said.

He didn't answer.

She couldn't believe how easily persuaded she'd been, allowing him to take the driver's seat so that she could lie back for a little in the passenger one because she 'looked upset'. Well, she was well and truly upset now. She'd expected an apology, some kind of explanation. Instead, the moment her eyes closed he'd turned the key, letting the powerful engine move them quietly down the lane away from the newly arrived police cars and everyone else towards the open road.

'Trust me,' he'd said, 'I'll explain in a moment.'

A great many moments had now come and gone. She didn't feel they had done something criminal exactly, but she suspected the police would not be best pleased. Most of all she disliked his assumption that he was in control. Perhaps that was what Dina found attractive in him, but she certainly didn't.

'D'you hear me? Stop the car now.'

'I'd rather not, but feel free to ask me anything else.'

His voice was so untroubled, so bloody carefree, she felt as if she was biting into candyfloss.

'What're you doing?' he glanced at her.

She was unzipping her bag. 'I'm phoning the police.'

'No, not now,' he stopped her with his left hand, grasped the bag and dropped it into the back of the car.

She was so angry she couldn't speak. Who the hell did he think he was?

'Is this the way you always handle a crisis? Dina's upset and confused, and you've just made everything worse.' He tried to talk over her protests, but she was having none of it. 'You should have been comforting her instead of going after that foreign man. I knew she'd be all right. He told me that, twice. But then you jump in, and start behaving like the playground bully. That man was merely trying to explain . . .'

'Your secretary has nothing to do with any of this. I met her yesterday for the first time.'

'But you said . . .'

'I'm sorry. No, just listen to me. This is complicated, so you'll have to bear with me.' They were approaching a speed camera. He glanced at the speedometer and slowed. 'I met Dina at your house yesterday. My colleague and I were there, dear lady, to protect you, to prevent you from being kidnapped.'

'Kidnapped?'

'We were waiting for them, but her unexpected arrival messed everything up. My priority remains the same, so I'm not going to stop until we've put a little more distance between us. All right?'

Did the foreign man really want to kidnap her? She sat back into her seat. Was this possible?

'You're a very important person, Miss Arbanisi.'

The great emerald sparkled at her, the only constant light in the present confusion.

'But he gave me this. It's the Sisi emerald.'

'It certainly is. He'd have taken it back from you soon enough. I'm sure you know your Macbeth, Miss Arbanisi. *Sometimes to win us to our harm, the instruments of darkness tell us truths.*'

117

'If you're not a friend of Dina's, who are you?'

'I can't tell you that, not just yet. You'll have to trust me. But I assure you, I'm not her boyfriend. Men in my line of work aren't good boyfriend material, I'm afraid. I had to say something when I was trying to find out what had happened to her. And I had to have some powerful justification for wanting to come here with you, when you said you'd been told to come alone. She's a nice girl, I'm sure, but not exactly my type.'

'Well I'm not having the police chase me halfway across the country. Turn the car round.'

'You're not thinking clearly.'

'I'm thinking very clearly. Turn round please.' She didn't care whether Dina was his type or not. She'd lost patience. All this about-turning and confusion and nonsense, she'd had more than enough.

He pulled off the road into the first convenient place, a tractor entry into a field, and switched off the engine.

'Miss Arbanisi,' he paused for a moment, as if he was considering exactly what to say, 'let me elaborate. First of all, this conversation isn't happening. You asked who I was. The short answer is, I don't exist. And I work for people who don't like it to be known that they exist either.'

She had to stop herself from laughing out loud. It sounded exactly like something out of a TV series or an airport paperback thriller.

'The man who was stabbed in your house was my colleague, Dan Reid. We've worked together for about three years. Try to imagine how I felt when I came to and found him. And your secretary had been taken hostage. The last thing I wanted was police involvement. Don't you realise how very important you are?'

It was said with such intensity, she had to look away.

The police still assumed there was only one burglar. Now he was telling her . . . what exactly was he telling her? The foreign man had been waiting for her, Dina had arrived instead, and he and another man had intervened?

'How could he have known I was going to come home?'

'He was waiting. You would have come home eventually.'

She supposed so.

'And the two of you knew he was there, waiting for me.'

'Exactly.'

'But who was the burglar? They took valuable stuff . . .'

'There wasn't a burglary. He wanted it to look like a burglary. You're the object of value.'

Irene felt very odd. She had never felt ordinary, not in the way that other people were. She'd always had so many dreams clamouring to be realised, yet she'd held back, afraid she'd not be understood. Even in the middle of the most exciting project, something was always lacking, something inside her. Inside her soul, it was as if she lived in a world with only two dimensions, a landscape of dull colours, half-heard sounds and false power. Now she was on the brink of something real, something wild and frightening and glorious.

'We're not playing games, Miss Arbanisi. That man with the scarred face is a ruthless killer. Fortunately the other one's not nearly so dedicated.'

'Which other one?'

'The one travelling with us in the boot.'

'What!'

'Oh, don't worry, he can't hurt you. But if he wakes up and starts thumping . . .'

'Why is he in the . . .?'

'I put him there. He was at the tower. I believe he'd gone to relieve himself. I'm not altogether sure what to do with him. Use him as bait, I think. If that fails, I'll have to think

119

of something else. Maybe I'll just let him go. I'm so sorry. I've shocked you with all this, haven't I?'

He had taken her hand.

'Why would anyone want to kidnap me?' she said. How squeaky she sounded, like a hysterical teenager. Being told she was important was one thing. But the thought that someone was intent on hurting her was unnerving.

'I don't have a lot of money,' she said, forcing her voice down. This wasn't exactly true, she reflected. It was just that she'd always considered that other people, including those she worked for, generally had a lot more cash in hand.

'I only know what I'm told. But anyone who wants to get to you is going to have to deal with me first. That much I promise you.'

Chapter Twenty-Five

Dina got out of the car and, opening the rear passenger door, took her two plastic bags and began walking towards the main road. Thank God. No more crazy driving. No more imminent death experiences. With a sigh of relief he followed her, but he was in no hurry to catch up. They'd covered quite a distance in their mad escape, and the tower was a long way off, but he thought it was pretty much a straight road back. She couldn't get lost.

He'd assumed they were in the middle of nowhere but once he reached the main road he saw that there was a small building on the other side. She'd crossed over and was now going inside. He shook his head. What the hell was she playing at now?

On the grass outside the building stood a sign. *Teas Coffees Light Snacks.* The lettering was hand-painted. It looked like an ordinary small house which had been transformed into a place to eat. The door tinkled as he went in. There was a counter with glass shelves, a large glass-fronted fridge with bottles, and half a dozen tables, covered with red cloths. A dark wood long-case clock stood against the end wall. Two women in white bib aprons were busy behind the counter. The air was fragrant with coffee and the sweet smell of warm bread.

'My friend . . .' he began, his hand gesturing half way up his chest.

'She's in the ladies' room,' one of the woman said, gesturing to a door.

He sat down near the door, next to an unlit fireplace. Across the room in a window alcove, was a curly-headed child in a high chair. An old woman and a younger one were adoring him. The young one was noticeably pregnant. Grandmother and daughter, he thought. A man in a red checked shirt, sleeves rolled, sat at another table, studying an unfolded map. Heavy walking boots and a large rucksack. Not police.

A boy in a dark blue apron emerged through a curtain of bright plastic strips. He stopped at the table.

Feliks said, 'We will have coffee, please. And water. And something to eat. What do you have? Something smells very good.'

He sounded just like his first English primer. How odd to be using those phrases at last.

The boy said he thought it might be the cheese scones. Though he wasn't sure what these were, Feliks asked him to bring some. The police might come at any time, but he was hungry and thirsty, and the smells had settled it.

'Would you be wanting cups or mugs?'

'What is the difference?'

'Mugs are bigger.'

'Mugs, then. Thank you.'

A few more years, he thought. *When you've been around for a few more years, boy, you won't stare at faces like mine. You'll master the quick sideways look – the controlled, polite glance that comes with maturity. That sweet, white-haired grandmother over there, she did it perfectly.*

When Dina emerged he caught her lightly by the arm. 'I've ordered coffee,' he said.

She didn't struggle. She looked exhausted, but her face

was clean, her hair tidied, and her hands and nails had been washed.

She said nothing. Her eyes were fixed on the trio at the window, as if she wished she could change places with the young mother.

Bottled water was brought, and glasses with ice, and coffee in tall white mugs. A jug of hot milk, butter in small silver foil packets just like the ones on the plane, and with them a plate bearing four large round fragrant cake-like objects, flecked with orange.

Behind them an old clock on the mantelpiece began to chime. Four times for the half hour.

'This is very fine coffee,' Feliks told her. No response. She wouldn't even look at him. Would she feel differently about him if by some magic he could turn back time, go back to who he'd once been, or swop faces with the endearing Lazslo, or the even more lovely smoothly-suited burglar? His grandmother would have had an incantation to do such a thing, she'd had them for every other ailment. Lighted match after lighted match, dropped into a bowl of water till some subtle alteration in the hissing satisfied her that evil had been dealt with. He could not imagine the old lady at the window, so clean-looking in her flowered dress and white cardigan, doing any such thing.

He poured milk into her mug, stirred in sugar, pushed it closer to her. After a few seconds she lifted it to her mouth.

'You should eat too.'

'I'm not hungry.'

'You will feel better with some food inside you.'

Warily he tasted some of the cheese bread. It was delicious. He broke one of the rounds in half and put them on her plate. How surreal all this was. Any moment the door would open and this illusion of normality would end. Possibly this was why the bread and the coffee tasted so good.

123

Each passing car seemed faster and more furious than the last. Hard, gleaming shells, with soft bodies inside, they boomed past, like so many crustaceans hurtling across the surface of an alien world.

'How did you get the car keys?' he asked. He wanted to ask why she had run, but it seemed better to begin elsewhere.

'I left them. They're in the ignition.'

'No, how did you first get them?'

It took her a moment to recall. 'They were lying on the grass.'

'When you and Miss Arbanisi first left the building, did you see Lazslo?'

She shook her head. The coffee seemed to please her, now that she'd tasted it.

'But the keys were on the ground? Was this before or after the police arrived?'

'Before. I saw them when Irene went back to speak to you.'

It made no sense. Why would Lazslo leave on foot? If the keys were so easy to spot, why hadn't Lazslo seen them?

'Something has happened to him. I was thinking he saw the police and hid somewhere or ran away, but whatever happened, it was before that.'

'When Irene came with that man?'

He nodded.

'But he could easily have run away before that,' she suggested. 'He wasn't . . . He didn't seem . . .'

Happy? No, Lazslo hadn't seemed happy. And from the look on her face, it seemed possible that Lazslo might have mentioned his unhappiness, as if he'd had a great deal to say for himself in the times when they'd been alone together.

124

'You felt sorry for him? And you believe everything he told you, of course. What did he say about me, I wonder.'

'Nothing, really.'

She was a poor liar.

'Let me explain something, Miss MacLeod. In my country, when I was conceived, it was still legal to have an abortion. But it was not legal by the time Lazslo was born.'

'What's that got to do with anything?'

'Lazslo was unplanned, and unwanted. His family was poor, and there were too many children already. He has always known this. He was given to his grandparents when he was three or four, and they were only a little less poor, so they begrudged every meal they gave to him. This was not uncommon,' he added, watching the small distressed changes in her listening face. 'There are many in my generation bitter in their hearts, because their parents told them the truth.'

'Why are you telling me all this?'

Why *was* he telling her? Lazslo's childhood miseries had nothing to do with the present situation. What did it matter if Lazslo had portrayed himself as the victim and Feliks as the villain? He cut the second cake in half and added butter, but the little rectangle was too cold to spread properly.

Unable to leave the silence alone, he went on, 'Lazslo and I used to be school mates. He was a little younger, but we played a lot of football together. They made me Captain, in fact, but I wasn't very good. I ran about a lot, but I never knew where the ball was. And I fell over a lot. Mostly over my own feet.'

'My sixth year report said, 'Donaldina still has to find her sport."

'Donaldina?'

'My name. It's a Highland thing. Traditional among the Gaels. I was supposed to be a boy.'

'It's a pretty name.'

'God, you must be the only person in the world who thinks so.'

She wiped crumbs away from her mouth, then said abruptly, 'Now I need to go to the toilet. I'm not going to do anything stupid, I just didn't go before. Ok?'

Just as the door swung shut behind her, he heard a car draw in to the small space at the front of the building. It might be the police. It might be Miss Arbanisi and the suited man. It might be no one at all. He took out his wallet, extracted notes enough to cover the bill and laid them in the middle of the table. Then he wiped his own mouth clean of crumbs with a paper napkin, got back into his jacket and zipped it up.

The man who entered was the man who had stood talking with the guard at the castle. In his mid to late thirties, clean-shaven and fit-looking, with close-cropped dark hair. He wore blue jeans. Sunglasses with gold rims dangled by one leg from the neck of his navy sweatshirt. He met Feliks's eye, nodded, and came over to the table.

'Can we have a word?' he asked.

Chapter Twenty-Six

The toilet was clean, but small. No manufacturer's name. She'd collected toilets as a child, calling out to her mother, 'It's a Twyfords, Mummy,' or whatever it was. Paul was terribly enthusiastic about bathrooms and toilets. There were around two hundred and forty different manufacturers of toilets in the UK, apparently. 'Memorise that, Dina. It's bound to come up in a pub quiz sometime,' he said. So she had, but it hadn't yet.

There was room in this one to sit down, stand up and turn around, but anyone over a size sixteen would have had serious problems. The urgent business done, she let her sore hands soak in hot water again for several minutes. What had possessed her to mention her failure at sport? How unreal it had been, talking to him like that, eating cheese scones as if nothing was wrong, as if they were just two ordinary people, passing the time.

He'd almost sounded sorry himself for Lazslo, the one who had nothing good to say about *him*. And he'd said her name was pretty. No one in the world had ever said that. Maybe she'd been a bit harsh, calling him a headless chicken. *God help me, the only man who's ever told me my name was pretty, and he has to be a priest.*

Not great, she thought, studying her reflection, but it would do. Whatever happened would happen, she told herself, but at least she looked less like a fool. She'd never reach the heights of Irene's elegance, but at least she looked clean.

Irene. How could she have lost sight of Irene? Where was she? Why had she left them? On the other hand, she was probably all right. Irene was a take-charge person. Irene didn't panic, she let other people do the panicking. She would be all right. It was not knowing, that was the problem.

Feliks wasn't at the table. Wasn't anywhere.

One of the women behind the counter smiled at her and pointed to the door. She went outside. There he was. Another man with him. They both turned at the sound of the door. Feliks held out something, a small laminated card.

'He says his name is Frank Gibson. He says he works for a newspaper.'

She looked at the card without seeing it.

'I want your story,' the dark-haired man said. 'I want the exclusive. The scoop. That's how I make . . .'

'I told you. There is no story here,' Feliks interrupted him.

'Trust me, I'm naughty. I listen in to the police frequencies. I'm willing to help you, if you promise to fill me in on the parts . . .'

'Leave us alone. We don't need help."

'Look, why don't you and the lady talk it over?' the man said, and he moved a few yards away.

Feliks ran his hand over his face and forehead, disordering his hair. 'What do you want to do?' he asked.

'Me? Am I making the decisions now?'

'I did not say that. I ask what do you want. Do you believe him?'

'Do you?'

He shook his head. 'However I am asking myself, all this time, why are the police not here. And how has this man found us when they have not?'

She had no answer either.

'If I ask this fellow to let us use his phone, to telephone the police to come here for us, will you stay this time, until they come? We only do harm if we run anymore.'

The café's got a phone, we could have asked to use it, she thought, but perhaps he didn't want to involve other people, or upset them. Or possibly he wanted to save his battery.

'Could we try to phone Irene as well? Or first. I mean, if we can tell the police where she is, show them we're being helpful . . .'

'Yes, that is a good idea.'

Hopefully Irene would be all right, and everything would be cleared up. She said, 'I'm going to tell them none of it was your fault.'

'Good,' he said, reaching towards her hair. She stiffened, then relaxed as he held it out. A tiny green fly. He blew it off into the breeze.

'Such a pity,' he said.

'What?'

'That we cannot grow wings.'

Chapter Twenty-Seven

'Do you have a phone? We would like to make a call before we talk to you further,' he told the dark-haired man.

'No problem.'

To get a signal they had to clamber quite far up the high slope behind the building, right up to a barbed wire fence. The reporter waited beside his car, not even watching them.

'Better you should talk to them. Sometimes I am slow with the accents,' he said.

'Could I just try Irene first?'

Why not? There was a breeze up here, bending the grass, blowing her hair into her eyes. She turned to face into it. He found a smooth place on a nearby boulder, and watched her. He liked it that she had thought of Irene. She was irrational, vain and most irritating, but there was some good in her. The sun moved behind a cloud. He zipped his jacket higher. This country was cold at its heart.

'It's just the answering message,' she said.

'Try again. Ask where she is, and say that we need her. Say we have a car.'

'Do we?'

'In a fashion,' he pointed to the reporter below.

At last. 'This is Dina,' the girl said, repeating it more loudly. But her face crumpled.

'What is wrong?' He got up from his rock.

'It's him,' she mouthed. She meant the suited blond fellow. It was the possibility he'd been refusing to consider.

'No, they're not,' the girl answered. Then, reluctantly, 'Yes, he is.'

'He wants you,' she held out the phone.

'How clever of you to find this number.' His enemy's voice was so close, as if he was right there. 'Dina tells me that you haven't been stopped by the police. Is that true?'

'Let me speak to Miss Arbanisi,' Feliks said, putting a hand on the fence post to steady himself.

'I don't think so. She's right beside me, and she's safe now. You'll never get the chance to hurt a hair of her head.'

'I don't mean to hurt anyone. You are the one who does. Let me speak to her, right now.'

'Over my dead body, pal. And you can swear at me all you like, you'll never get her.'

Swear? When had he sworn?

'Who are you? Who are you working for? For my father?'

'Now you're talking sense. Of course we can meet. I was about to suggest it myself. Your colleague is with us, by the way. He was a little agitated, but he's fine now.'

Did he mean Lazslo? Why was Lazslo with them?

'That won't be possible, sorry.'

What wouldn't be possible? He hadn't said anything. The man was crazy.

'Listen to me. We are about to speak to the police. If you harm Miss Arbanisi or my colleague . . .'

'Oh, bad, bad idea. Don't do that. Don't speak to them. Drive north. Phone us again in an hour, and we'll arrange somewhere to meet. And bring Miss MacLeod with you, unharmed.'

'She has nothing to do with this.'

'Miss Arbanisi wants to be sure you haven't maltreated her in any way before I let you have your friend back.'

131

'But she is here. She can talk to Miss Arbanisi now. She is free to do whatever she likes . . .'

The phone went dead.

'What did he say? Is she with him? Is she all right?'

He'd been gripping the wire. A line and two small puncture wounds dotted his palm.

'He talks like a crazy man, then he talks sense. I don't understand it. He tells me to drive north . . .'

'North? Why?'

'I don't know. He says he has Lazslo too.'

'No.'

'He says they are both all right.' But it might all be lies. Lazslo and Miss Arbanisi could be dead or dying . . .

"You're bleeding," she said.

He sucked his hand briefly, passing the phone to her, and held his palms together.

'What are we going to do?' she asked at last.

What could he tell her? He had absolutely no ideas in his head, except one. The man so good-looking, so well-dressed, so strange in conversation was, exactly as he'd suspected, a man completely lacking in conscience. As a teenager, he'd watched one or two try to attach themselves to his father. They made a strong impression, then they just weren't around anymore. Dimitar had explained why. Boris recognised the risks they posed. According to Dimitar, there were some men, and women too, in the world who were by nature indifferent to beauty and ugliness, goodness and evil. 'There is no loyalty in them,' he'd signed, 'nor can they change.'

'We should not accept this man's help,' Feliks said, looking down to the journalist. 'No matter what he says he is.'

She was wilting, he saw, like a plant too long without light.

'We can let him take us back to our car. All right?'

He supported her on the way down the rock-strewn slope, and this time she seemed content to take his arm.

Chapter Twenty-Eight

Lazslo cradled his arms around his aching head in the boot of the stranger's car. They had stopped for a few moments, but all too soon they were moving again. So the end was not yet. They would have to stop sometime, he told himself. Although it was undeniable that a car could stop in all sorts of ways. A car could be left to rust in the middle of a forest. A car could be set on fire, or pushed over a bridge into an icy stream.

He couldn't recall a time when he'd been more miserable. Not that he was really surprised. It was the story of his entire life. Bad timing, being in the wrong place at the wrong time, doing what he was told because he had no choice. If the blond man had come alone, or dressed in workman's clothes as he had been before, he would have known what to do. But to see him stepping out of the Lexus, all smiles, with an elegant beautiful woman on his arm, just as he himself emerged with his pants half-zipped, that had been a filthy rotten trick on the part of Fate.

She'd disappeared into the tower, and the man had waved to him.

'How are you? No problem finding the place? So sorry about the mix-up yesterday,' the man had begun, taking his arm, but within a split second, he'd produced a knife, urging Lazslo to be very good, and promising to do certain things with the knife if he was bad. And of course, of Feliks there had been no sign whatsoever. So now here he was, in pitch darkness, with an unbelievably sore stomach from the punch that had knocked the sense out of him before he'd been pushed into the boot. He'd felt all around inside the space the best he could to see if there was anything that could help him. There was a small holdall, leather by the smell of it. It contained clothes, a woman's clothes, underwear that felt like silk. There was something attached to the underside of the boot lid, a small, metallic, square thing. It came away easily. He put it in his pocket in case it might prove useful.

Judging from the gentle swaying and the lack of traffic noise, they were now on a main road, but out in the countryside. Now and then they overtook something without using much acceleration. Clearly they were travelling faster than other cars. Were they being followed? Perhaps Feliks was following them. He'd managed to drop the keys to their own car in what he hoped was an obvious place at the edge of the grass. Suppose Feliks found them, and was now by some miracle following. It would take a miracle, since as far as Lazslo knew, he had never got his nerve back after the crash.

It was about time Feliks did something right. He'd brought the girl with them, instead of believing her story and letting her go. Stupid decisions every time. Of course it was possible that Feliks had also been caught, that he was a prisoner inside the car.

Abruptly they stopped. He hit the back wall. The daylight was momentarily blinding.

'Get out.'

He fell to his knees onto wet rutted earth. The man caught his collar and yanked him to his feet. The beautiful woman was standing a little distance away, staring straight ahead, as if none of this interested her. He glanced inside the car. No one else there. No traffic in sight either.

'Why are you . . .?' he began, but the blond man silenced him with a slap across the mouth.

'Move,' he ordered, pointing to a culvert under a stone arch. Once beneath it, the man said, 'Face against the wall, hands on your head.'

He did as he was told. The wall was wet, slimy with moss. He could taste blood, where the soft flesh of his inside lip had caught his teeth. The man tapped his head with what felt like the heavy end of the knife. He winced.

'Does it hurt? I do hope so. Your boyfriend keeps trying to hurt me every time we meet. Or were you the one who stabbed my colleague?'

'I only drive the car. I have no choice.'

The man laughed. 'Oh we always have a choice. From the moment those bright little sunbeams wake us every morning, we have a choice. For example, you could choose not to tell me a number of things I want to know. On the other hand, since they do make life so much easier, you could choose to keep all of your fingers.'

He was so close Lazslo could smell him. He was wearing scent, like a woman.

'Who are you working for?'

There didn't seem much point in lying.

'The President.'

'President of what?'

'My country.'

The man professed never to have heard of it. Was this a bluff, or did he really not know? There was no way to tell by his voice, which sounded English with no trace of an accent.

'It is between Bazakestan and the Soviets.'

Should he volunteer more information? Or was it safer to sound like an ignorant driver who barely spoke the language, who knew nothing of any importance? Which wasn't entirely false. 'Go with my son. Drive carefully. Remember everything. Do what he tells you,' Boris had told him. But no explanation of why the Arbanisi woman was important or what purpose her return might serve.

'How many are there of you?'

'Not many. Perhaps six millions.'

'*Here*, you fool. Who else is here with you?'

'Berisovic and I. That is all. He speak to people. I drive car. He cannot drive car. He has once a bad crash, he . . .'

'Forget the bloody car. That ring he gave her, is it real?'

'Ring? I don't know about a ring,' Lazslo began. Abruptly his jaw was caught, turned sideways. There was a swift sensation like a thread being drawn across his cheek, and a stinging pain.

'Keep them on your head!' the man snapped, as he dropped one hand to feel confusedly for his face. 'Not that your opinion matters,' he went on. 'The lady says it's real, and I suppose she's the type of lady who'd know. Closer to my heart at this moment is the matter of who you've told about yesterday. I'd like to know, before the police do. And please don't tell me you've told nobody, because I won't believe you.'

'Not me. Berisovic. He is a crazy man, he . . .'

'Who else knows what happened?'

'He does the talking. He doesn't tell me. I think maybe you must ask him.'

'Calm down, or you'll shake yourself out of your pants again. So, you're just the poor little man with no choice. Just the driver. You don't know what's going on, you should be safe at home in your own little bed? You must be wondering what the hell this is all about.'

'No, I don't ask . . .'

'You don't ask?'

'No. I just . . .'

'You just drive the car.' The man finished the sentence for him, with a short laugh.

'All right then, off you go.' He pulled Lazslo round.

He stared, not understanding.

'You can leave. I mean it. I don't want you. As far as I'm concerned you can disappear. As long as you tell no one about our little chat. You'd better get moving if you want to reach civilisation before dark. Off you go.' He gestured to a track that led out from under the culvert, landward, away from the road.

Bewildered, Lazslo began to walk, stumbling a couple of times over the hummocky grass in the middle of the track. He managed a cigarette out of the pack and lit it without stopping. Where the track forked, he took the higher one, which led into a sparse birch wood. The trees gave way to bracken. The way rapidly grew steeper until he began to feel his heart pumping, but he didn't stop, until finally he found himself with nowhere to go, high above the dark grey ribbon of a road. He couldn't tell if he was ahead of the place where the car had stopped, or behind it, or even if this was a different road entirely. It didn't matter. At some point he would have to think about what mattered and what didn't, but not yet.

On the far side of the road a movement caught his eye. A goshawk, he thought at first, but really it was too small. It settled on a telegraph pole, and looked at him, then almost at once flew away. He'd liked birdwatching at home, and Grandma encouraged it. She liked him out of the house. He'd kept a notebook for a time, with drawings. Honey Buzzards with their white black-spotted breasts, different woodpeckers, Spotted Eagles, and all the songbirds, Goldcrests, Firecrests, Crossbills, Serins. His first set of coloured pencils had been wonderful, then immediately annoying, because the colours weren't right for the actual

137

colours. Eagles, he recalled, could see eight times better than people, but they failed in their hunting almost three quarters of the time, which was . . .

Something hit his head, and he was falling, tumbling down, crashing into bushes and boulders till he hit hard ground. He couldn't move, though the world itself was moving in circles. Worse than the pain was the strange overwhelming heaviness. He tried to speak, but no sound came out, and the feebleness of his mouth frightened him. All that came to him was the after-image of the hawk. It worried him that he couldn't name it: he could so clearly picture its wings spread against the sky. He'd known the names of so many birds when he was eight. First prize in the Nature Test. But of course, this was a foreign bird. They couldn't fault him for failing to recognise a foreign bird, could they? The pain in his back was the worst. Slowly the idea came to him that the blond man might not have let him go, might have in fact followed him ever so quietly through the wood and bracken. This was not the way it should be. This wasn't right. He deserved more time. A beginning had been made back at the meeting place. With more time, he could make Feliks listen, make him understand. Feliks would forgive him, trust him, share confidences as they had in the past.

Am I dying? he wondered.

I don't know how to do this, he thought worriedly, as the pinpoints of light faded, *I don't know what to do.*

Chapter Twenty-Nine

Irene grew tired of fresh air, and got back into the car. Automatically she checked in the mirror for stray hairs. There was nothing else to do then but stare out at the bleak moorland. In the fading sunlight it was a miserable, uninviting expanse of greenish grey.

Pulling in to the side of the road, he'd got to her handbag first and answered the call.

'Who is it?' she'd asked.

'Our other foreign friend,' he'd whispered. 'Don't worry, my dear. I'll take care of this,' he'd told her, as if he was used to locking people in the boots of cars. As if it was nothing. And now there was no sign of either of them, and she couldn't do a thing because he'd taken the bloody keys with him.

She'd been shocked by the brutal way he slapped the man. But what should she have done? If he was telling the truth, all the talk about the home country was meant to deceive her. These foreign men intended to hurt her. How passionate he'd sounded, telling them he'd never let her be harmed.

She studied the ring. Impossible to guess how much it might be worth, but in any case, she would never part with it. It was so very, very beautiful. Emeralds were full of good luck. In the old tales, they protected you from evil spirits. They were meant to protect your chastity, she remembered. A little late for that.

The minutes dragged on. The inside of the car began to feel distinctly chilly. There were cars passing, not many, but some. Should she try to stop one? She could say that she'd broken down, and ask to be taken to civilisation. A glass of hot lemon tea would be heaven. She was on the brink of getting out again when Charles reappeared. Of the foreign man there was no sign.

How well he moved. His legs curved ever so slightly outwards, ugly in a woman, but so appealing in a man.

'All right?' he asked.

'No. Where is he? What did you do with him?'

'Oh, I let him go.'

'What!'

'He doesn't know anything. He's harmless.'

'You said he was dangerous. You said he wanted to kill me.'

He'd already started the car. He pulled out onto the road, accelerating fast. 'Are you feeling hungry?' he said. 'We've missed lunch, but there must be somewhere around here where we can get a quick bite.'

'How could he be harmless? Does that mean the other one's harmless too?'

'I'm sorry?'

'You said the one with the scar wanted to assassinate me. I don't understand how you can know that and let this one go. I really think we should stop and call the police, in case he – '

'I'm sorry. Please don't be angry. This isn't easy for me. I'm making this up as we go along – there should have been two of us, remember. There's just no way I can explain all this to you right now. But I will, once everything calms down. Once I get your little secretary back, we'll all have time to sit down and talk. I'm not forgetting about her.'

Was this a reproach? She wasn't sure she liked his tone.

Nor did she like being told to wait. She hadn't been told to wait since she'd stood in the queue to go into class at Primary School. Briefly she considered Dina. It was frustrating not knowing what was happening. Oh well, what could she do? Dina had got herself into a mess, and would have to get herself out of it.

His skin had a lot of irregularities. Tiny little pockmarks. Either she hadn't noticed or they were more obvious than before. She wondered if he'd been using a concealer, which had now been sweated or rubbed off. How satisfying. It was a tiny bit comforting to know that someone who spent his life ordering people in and out of car boots had flaws.

'What was that?' she exclaimed, startled by a pale brown heap at the side of the road.

'Roadkill. Poor thing. Fallow deer, from the size of it. And by the way, the one I just let go, he wasn't the one who killed your cat. I questioned him about that.'

After a few moments she found herself in tears. Poor beautiful Bebe. She hadn't seen the body, would never have to remember him dead. When she pictured him, she would always see him as she'd last seen him, lying on the window ledge, licking his paws, the sun making his creamy fur luminous.

He dropped a handkerchief on her knee, then took hold of her right hand. His was cool, smooth and reassuring. As the miles passed, and his hand remained lightly around hers, she began to regret her earlier anger and her unseemly glee at his skin problems. He said nothing at all, as if he knew that words didn't help when women cried. She liked him the better for it.

Chapter Thirty

When Feliks woke, they were still moving but the world had turned grey. He checked his watch and cursed silently. Nearly an hour gone. He hadn't intended to close his eyes at all.

'Why did you let me sleep?' he asked. 'We need to make the phone call.'

'I know that. I was watching the time. Have some chocolate.'

'Where did that come from?'

'Frank gave it to me before we left.'

Meaning the reporter. He'd not protested when they told him they had nothing to say. He'd driven them back to the deserted warehouse without even asking what they intended to do. 'It's you the police are interested in, not her. You do realise that,' he'd said, too low for Dina to hear.

'Of course. She is innocent.'

'So why are you taking her with you?'

'I'm not forcing her to do anything.'

The man had shrugged.

Feliks wondered now if he was the one who'd tried to follow them out of the city, but said nothing. He hadn't been paying that much attention, confident that Lazslo would lose whoever it might be. Lazslo would have known, number plate and driver both.

He checked his phone. No reception. This was all going on too long. Maybe the reporter had been right.

'We'll need petrol soon,' she said. 'Have you got any money left?'

'There is plenty. Could you stop somewhere along here?'

She did as she was bid.

'Move over,' he told her, getting out and walking round to the driver's seat which she obediently vacated.

'Now get out, please.' He drew out his wallet and extracted several large denomination notes. 'I apologise about this, but I have to leave you.'

'There's nothing here,' she protested.

'I cannot help that. You will be safer here than you will be with me.'

'No I won't.'

'Take this, and get out. Do I have to throw you? You know I can do that.'

'He said you hated everyone, and he was right. You're horrible, and disgusting. I don't believe you were ever a priest!'

'You're right. I was never a priest. I just loved to get up before dawn, eat plain food, be cold all winter and sleep without a mattress. It was so disgusting and horrible it suited me perfectly.'

She grabbed the money and got out, slamming the door exactly as he expected her to.

A motorbike roared past. And another. Six seconds later, a third.

He counted the seconds, right up to ten, and nothing passed, and it was safe to pull out into the road, and still the fingers of his right hand refused to turn the key. When he got to eighteen she was opening the driver's door.

He got out and let her in. He walked round to the passenger side and took his former place.

Without a word, she started the car and they moved off.

He saw the next speed camera sign as an alien, a square head with a striped neck, one big eye and one little eye. It seemed to watch him as they passed, trying to read his thoughts.

They swung through a small village, with no one on its main street, and quickly out again into increasingly desolate countryside. White poles with pink tops marked the road. Snow markers, he guessed. Some sloped sideways, as if they'd been struck by passing cars. Away to the left one small tree was growing out of a boulder. Little else grew here, only straw-coloured grass, and clumps of old heather. Grey rock and pools of water, and mountains in the far distance.

Something was happening on the road. The cars in the distance ahead seemed to be slowing, their warning lights on. 'It'll be a tractor probably,' she said, 'or sheep being moved. Normal happenings in this part of the world. Just as well it's not rutting season or stags would be falling on us out of the hills. It's most likely another geriatric caravan.'

'Geriatric?' he said.

'People retire from work and go travelling in them. The older they get, the bigger the caravan and the slower they drive. Or else it's motorhomes.'

It was impossible to see the cause of the delay. The road curved with low hills on the right, and the moor on their left. She edged forward in second gear.

'No, I think they are stopping the cars,' he said.

There was nowhere to go without making a dangerous u-turn. She was looking at the petrol gauge. Should he leave her, try to make his way somehow on foot?

'What do you want to do? The nearest petrol is ahead of us,' she said.

He tried the phone again. Still no signal. They rounded the next bend. There was a little cluster of cars on the narrow left-hand verge, and a truck parked on the right, its nearside wheels in the ditch. Men were controlling traffic in both directions, stopping cars, waving them on. Ordinary men, he thought, although one wore an orange jacket. He couldn't see any police cars. She was very calm. Surprising. Maybe she was one of those people who could shut things into compartments in their minds. Or perhaps she was so used to normality that the last couple of days seemed to her like a temporary aberration that would soon be put right. He still hadn't asked her why she'd run from the police. And he was making things worse, making use of her, taking her further from the safety she deserved.

What did you expect? You fail every woman in your life.

Hiding in his bedroom, hardening his heart, reading Wild West stories behind the striped green curtains, with the cold glass of the window against his spine. Pretending to hear nothing but the whoop of Indians, the crack of cowboy guns, to feel only the heat of campfires burn his cheeks. Hardening his heart. Refusing to hear his mother crying.

What could I do? I was only a child.

But later? When you were taller than he was? When you began to doubt him? If you didn't see it, did that mean it wasn't happening?

And Anna. More devotion he hadn't deserved but had done nothing to discourage, even though he knew it was dangerous for her to boast about having him in the group.

Because it pleased me.

He stared at the barrenness surrounding them. A strange, melancholy landscape. Looking out of the plane, he'd been struck by how green this country was, how ordered its landscape compared to those at home, but here in the north there was little to please the eye. Low wiry bushes, and boulders and towering hills. The sky had grown dull, one all-covering mass of grey.

I am perverse. I only want what I have no right to have.

If the journalist was correct, if this was in fact a police roadblock for him, he would go to them, not crawl forward, waiting to be hauled out in view of all these people. Better to get it done. There had been too much running and hiding and stupidity. Without warning her, he exited the car, and walked quickly towards the tall, red-faced man in the orange jacket.

'Who is in charge here?' he asked.

'Not me, pal. There's been a bad accident. And here's the rain now.' He held his hand palm up. 'Just what we need.'

'Are there no police here?'

'On their way, I think.'

Feliks looked back at the girl. In the stationary line, it seemed every occupant of every car was straining to see what was going on. Only a few cars were being let through at a time. The air was tainted with exhaust fumes, thrumming with frustrated engines. There was a bearded man in a bright butter-yellow shirt on his knees beside a prone figure. Beside him, on a strip of weeds at the foot of the rocky outcroppings, lay a bicycle, with a pony-tailed fellow crouching over its chain. A middle aged woman with unnaturally red hair stopped him, barred his way.

'There's nothing to look at. Go back to your car please.'

'What is wrong?'

Then he saw the protruding boots, recognised the shape and colour. A blue and green checked rug covered most of Lazslo's trunk. For a split second he hesitated, then, ignoring her and other voices around him, he went forward.

'I know him,' he said, pushing away hands that tried to stop him. Voices buzzed like disturbed wasps round his head.

146

'Lazslo. Can you hear me? What happened? Lazslo, speak to me. Wake up.'

He said none of it in English, bending down closer to the bruised, bleeding face.

'Who is he? D'you know him?'

'What language is that?'

'Don't move him.'

'Leave him alone, you're not helping.'

They were all speaking at once.

He stood up, and the people didn't make any move to stop him. At the car he motioned for her to roll the window down.

'He's dying. I should never have let him come. He trusted me and now he's dying.'

She stared up at him.

'It's Lazslo. I think he's dying,' he told her, in English this time. The words were even emptier in this alien language. Flat, senseless noises with no meaning. Butter. Why was he thinking of butter? Suddenly he remembered. It was his birthday. Laughing, drinking too much beer, the whole crowd huddled together for warmth like winter birds. Or like penguins, someone said, though none of them had ever seen a live one. Lazslo arrived late with an oblong shape in white paper, tied with brown string. He'd missed classes, waited for hours in a queue, and when Feliks took off the wrapping paper to reveal the bright, beautiful slab of yellowness everyone had applauded, slapping Lazslo on the back. He'd blushed, overcome by their approval. 'Squirrel! Squirrel!' they had chanted. Viktor had composed one of his instant poems, honouring Lazslo's achievement, declaiming it upside down, his huge hairy feet planted like bizarre white fungi against the wall.

You didn't deserve this, Lazslo. Not even for the years you spent kissing Janek's bum.

Chapter Thirty-One

He'd closed his eyes. The rain was darkening the pale brown of his jacket. His fists were clenched in his pockets. She wanted to know what exactly had happened, but didn't dare.

'I will go back and stay with him. They have already sent for the police.'

Why am I doing this? Why do I want to help him?

So, what would you do, if he was yours to help, Dina? Get rid of the beard, buy him some nice aftershave? Would you insist on plastic surgery too, to make him beautiful?

From out of nowhere, Grandfather MacLeod's voice came, reverberating in the Gaelic, 'Charm is deceitful and beauty is vain, but a woman who fears the Lord is to be praised'.

And there he was, all of a sudden, on the road before her, as on one particular day when as a child she'd seen him, walking down the main street, walking slowly down the exact middle of it, in his relentless, tight-brimmed hat, defying all the cars, because it was the Sabbath, and people had no business to be driving. The locals, who knew the way he would take, avoided those streets at that hour, or bullishly drove without moderating their speed (though they kept well in to the side). Tourists, who didn't know who he was, and therefore presumed he was insane, slowed, swerved, or waited. Those few who agreed with him respected him for it; the rest of the world called it arrogance. She'd never been able to decide. Still didn't want to. Because this was the same man who told her she was the apple of his eye, who secreted mini-packets of Smarties in his study and smiled with delight when she found them after many hints of getting colder or hotter.

She'd have to move the car, but he refused to get back in.

'Well, you could sit down on one of those rocks under the banking,' she suggested, 'where there's a bit of shelter. I'll park a bit further on.'

The rock he chose was too high. She couldn't get up. If she did, her feet would dangle like a child's. He didn't sit, but leaned against it, so she did too. His head was down, chin on his chest. The rain grew heavier. She suggested again, in vain, that they go back to the car. He wanted to stay where he could see what was happening.

Later she would ponder how different things might have turned out if she had gone back herself, or asked questions or even spoken at this point, if she'd been her usual stupid, thoughtless self and twittered on because she wanted to know everything.

'I think he was afraid all of his life,' he said. 'Always unsure, always looking about him. We used to say he was waiting for the sky to fall. In the practices, at school, he could score goals, and we kept hoping he would, but in a real game it just never happened. But there were some things he could do really well. He could fix machines. From quite young. Mechanical things, a pump, or a boiler, you know? People used to ask him to come and fix things. And he could remember everything. He could look at a diagram. Wiring, circuits, the plan of a building, he could see it all in his mind. I don't know where this talent came from. They said his parents were as dull as wood. He should not have been here. He was afraid to refuse Boris. If I'd known I could have objected.'

'Who is Boris?' she said.

'My father. He is still the President of our country. How, I don't know. He made Lazslo come with me.'

'Because you were friends.'

He let out a short, sour sound. 'Because he knew we were no longer friends. It is the kind of thing Boris likes to do, you know? Take two starving dogs, put them in the cage, then wait to see them tear each other's throats. Did Lazslo say we were friends?'

'I'm sorry, It's none of my . . .'

'I didn't have friends. They were my . . . my chess pieces, you know? To move and manipulate, to sacrifice for glorious democracy. It is very odd. I hated my father. I gave myself to everything he hated, but now I find I am exactly like him.'

Fearful of his mounting distress, she looked away, trying to frame some kind of answer, some kind of comforting word. Abruptly his hand was on her chin, and the fierce pressure of his mouth on hers made speech impossible.

'Is this a private session or can anyone join in?'

The journalist. Frank. Under a big golf umbrella. She was so dazed, so embarrassed and breathless, she couldn't say a word. Nor it seemed could Feliks. But he stood up and she was scared he was going to hit the other man, who must have thought the same thing, because he stepped back.

'I'm sorry, that was uncalled for,' the man said quickly. 'Miss MacLeod, you're drenched, take this,' It was the umbrella, black and white panels, a wooden handle. 'Go and sit in my car. It's not locked. You know which one.'

'Don't . . .' Feliks tried to stop her.

'Trust me, I'm a policeman,' Frank said. 'I'm on your

side, OK? Have mercy on her, man,' this to Feliks. 'She's soaking wet and shivering like a drowning lamb. Have some sense. Let her go.'

When she looked back, they were really close together, but not fighting. There was a red fleece rug bundled up on the back seat. She got in, putting the closed umbrella on the back shelf. The fleece smelled of fabric softener. She pulled it around herself, but the more she tried to stop shivering, the colder she felt. The outside world was a blur behind the rain-battered glass. Then after what seemed an age, the front passenger door opened and Feliks got in. He put the plastic bags from their own car on the back seat next to her. She waited and waited till she could wait no more.

'This is insane, he can't be a policeman, can he? What's he doing? Should we just be sitting here? And you were supposed to phone that man again. Are you going to phone him? If he's a policeman why hasn't he – '

'Stop!'

She stopped.

Chapter Thirty-Two

Frank got into the car and set it in motion.

'They've sent for an ambulance. He's unconscious, but he's breathing, so there's no need to despair.' No need for the harsh truth, Frank figured, when a lie would calm everyone down. 'There's a couple of chocolate bars in the side door. You take one, and give her one.'

'I demand you tell me who you are.'

'OK. No need to yell, I'll tell you all you want to know,' Frank said. 'You're scaring her,' he added. 'If I said that Dimitar sent his regards, would that reassure you?'

Berisovic's face changed, as if he'd been slapped.

'Let's just drive for a bit, shall we?' Frank said, and to his relief, there were no protestations. Berisovic passed chocolate to the girl but took none himself. There were mountains a short distance from the road on either side now, so bare and smooth they looked as if they might slide down at a given signal onto the narrow strip of tarmac. Sheep nibbled at sparse grass behind fencing.

When they'd gone a fair distance, he began, 'I'm not a reporter, but you knew that from the start, right? My apologies, Miss MacLeod.'

Time for the clincher. He glanced in the mirror, reduced speed to be on the safe side, then, from under the dashboard, pulled out a gun.

'This is real,' he held it up, 'but it's perfectly legal and I haven't had to use it for a long time. Here, you can have it.'

Berisovic exclaimed in surprise, and fumbling, dropped the weapon onto the floor.

'Don't worry, Miss Macleod, the safety's on.'

This time he made proper eye contact with her. *Convince her, convince him. Both or neither.* He spoke to Berisovic, but was careful to glance often at her in the mirror as he drove, keeping her with him.

'I am a policeman, of a sort. I work for . . . let's just say I work for people who want to make sure that you and Miss Arbanisi come home together.'

'Show me your identity card.'

'We don't carry one. This isn't America.' He didn't look down to see where the gun had gone. All this would only work if he put no pressure on Berisovic at all.

'Who is the man who has taken her?'

'I don't know yet, but it's being looked into.'

It annoyed him how slowly the desk boys worked, despite all the gadgetry at their disposal. He'd caught a glimpse of their strange world a few times. 'We don't let them meet normal human beings,' he'd been told. 'We just open the door and throw a few buns at them now and then.' Of course, they were all in the same boat; he couldn't tell normal human beings what he did either. Now and again, particularly when he was absent from Brenda and the boys for too long, he was becoming afraid that he too was merely part of a machine.

'How do you know Dimitar? You have conversed with him?'

Thin ice. All he knew was the name.

'Not personally.'

'How did he look? Has he cut his hair yet? I told him to cut it. It was a ridiculous length.'

'I don't know. Let's just say he's a friend of a friend.'

'An English friend? But I think his English is very poor. His accent is bad.'

'Yours is excellent. But then, you studied English Literature didn't you, when you were . . .'

'And have your friends spoken to my father also? Did he send his regards?'

This had to be stopped. Berisovic's voice was rising, his sarcasm edging into anger. 'Look, I'm not telling you what to do. You can do whatever you want. But if you trust me, we can work together, we can deal with the bastard who attacked your friend Cristescu and get the Countess back safely.'

Berisovic reached down, picked up the gun and pointed it at him. 'Bang,' he said loudly.

The girl squealed from the back seat. Frank braked, managed not to swerve. When nothing else happened, he gradually increased speed. It was getting late. He'd have to find somewhere to keep them overnight. Easy does it, old son, he told himself. One thing at a time. He's been through too much. His world's breaking apart. Give the man some hard facts to stick it back together.

'You don't really know why you're here, do you?' he said. 'The real reason you've to bring the Countess home? Let me tell you. One word. Oil.'

Berisovic said nothing. Did he know or not?

'Apparently there is a whole lot of it in your northern provinces. The Russians want the deal. Predictably, so do one or two others.'

'What has this to do with Miss Arbanisi?'

'Your father wants her support. It's all very touch and go. He wants the nationalists behind him, whatever decision he makes.'

'I was in the north. I heard nothing about this oil.'

'Only a few people have.'

'Including your friends. You are very coy about them. Is it the Americans?'

Berisovic was alternately looking down at the gun and back at him. With equal dislike, it seemed. But at least the rage had died. Clearly he was the sort who liked to have something to worry at, like a terrier at a rabbit hole, the kind of man who, whether he knew it or not, preferred questions to answers.

'Let's just say I'm on your side.'

'That is certainly a comfort. However, it is still strange to me that Boris sent *me* to bring her back, you know? Perhaps your employers know the answer to that also?'

'They might, but they don't tell me everything.'

Berisovic took time to digest this. Then another question occurred to him. 'And they don't know who is this man, this bastard we must track down?'

'They do not. I was hoping you could tell me. It's like he dropped in from the moon.'

'Have you tried asking Uncle Janek?'

'Who?'

'Never mind. Could I ask you to pull in here?'

'Here' was a small lay-by with a heap of gravel at the far end.

'Miss MacLeod, please stay in the car. Now, you will go to the rear,' Berisovic told him, gesturing with the gun. 'Leave the key where it is, please.'

Out of the car, Frank immediately noticed how the temperature had fallen. The rain had gone, but there was a cool wind. He glanced at their surroundings. Gorse bushes, growing through the usual wire fence. Further along the road on the brow of the next hill, a small white house with outbuildings. No washing on the line and no lights on. No way to tell if it was inhabited.

He had to be very careful. The last thing he needed was to have them wandering off to try to find the Countess and her kidnapper on their own. The girl wasn't a problem.

Berisovic was another matter. His antipathy to authority of any shape or colour was well-documented. But it was doable. With care Berisovic could be managed.

'You will go over that fence and begin to walk away from me.'

'Don't do this. You're scaring her again,' he said.

But Berisovic didn't so much as glance at the girl, whose face against the window evidenced shock and utter disbelief.

'You're not equipped to deal with this. You need me, especially with Cristescu out of it. Don't be ridiculous.'

'But I prefer to be ridiculous. Take your wallet and your phone out and throw them towards me. Be very careful how you remove them. Throw slowly. Good. Now the fence.'

Astride the wire, he tried again. 'Look, this is not going to do any good. There's more chance of us sorting things out together. I've already got the police off your back twice. Haven't you wondered why they've not caught up with you?'

He knew with a calm certainty that this posturing with the gun was all bluff. The next moment, he was on his back, spread-eagled in coarse wet gorse. The pain in his left leg was so intense he couldn't focus or right himself for several minutes, and even then he didn't believe what had happened. By the time he pulled his mind back from the void, the car and its two occupants had gone.

Chapter Thirty-Three

'This seems half decent.'

Irene looked at the building Charles was pointing to. He'd been complaining of hunger pangs for the last hour and a half, overtaking every car in sight. It didn't look like much to her, just a long white building close to the loch shore, but she didn't say anything.

When she stepped out into the rain, she was surprised by the salt tang in the air. Was this the sea, or a sea loch? She had no idea where they were.

'Where are we?' she asked. He went on ahead. The place looked rather run-down, despite the two AA stars on the wall. She followed him inside. No one at the reception desk. He was at the bar already, looking at a menu. The room was ghastly – low, dark and airless. Gold-framed paintings of highland cows standing in shallow water, muddy green wallpaper, subdued lighting. She felt herself struggling to breathe. Far, far worse was a stag's head on the opposite wall. Its woeful brown eyes stared at the room in search of some explanation.

'God, not here,' she said loudly. The few people at the low tables looked round at her. Was there perhaps somewhere else, Charles asked, less crowded? The barman suggested they might prefer the conservatory.

Here there was more light. The curtains lacked charisma, and the dark-stained wooden tables each had a brass number hammered into the surface, but one wall was completely window, and everything felt much cleaner. Outside, the afternoon light was recovering from the rain. They were very near the water's edge, separated from the shore only by a lawn, two Scots pines and a low drystone wall. The waves looked rough, but thanks to the double panes of glass they broke soundlessly on the shingle. On the far side of the water, a ridge of mountains went on without any visible end.

A very tall young waiter with ginger hair and absurd mutton chop whiskers materialised beside them. She said she didn't want anything, then, pressed by Charles, she ordered lemon tea. He took his time, finally deciding on lentil soup and a toasted cheese sandwich, exchanging pleasantries, asking about the local fishing. Apparently she and Charles were both keen on fishing.

At a corner table, a middle-aged couple were eating in silence with no sign of pleasure, looking at nothing. Grey tweed, grey faces, grey hair. Irene accessorized the woman with a deep rose silk scarf and matching earrings, gave her attractive white tones in the front of her hair, used make-up on her sad face, removed the laced shoes and gave her black patent ones with a large matching messenger bag. The man, she decided, was a lost cause.

Outside on the lawn, a boy with a bullet-shaped head was gathering twigs and other detritus, carrying them to a nearby wheelbarrow. A young girl in tight blue jeans appeared, holding a closed umbrella. She had good straight shoulders. Her shiny brown hair swung in a pony-tail. Watching how the girl angled her body towards the boy Irene felt a surge of annoyance. *No, not him,* she told the girl, *not this one. You can do so much better. Don't waste energy on this one. Not even for practice.*

The two of them walked away, the boy pushing the barrow.

Irene stood up. She felt old for the first time in her life.

'What's wrong? Where are you going?' Charles said. He caught her sleeve.

Where the hell did he think she was going? For a swim?

'I'm going to the loo. Is that allowed?'

The carpet throughout the place was Black Watch tartan. Absolutely typical. She hated tartan carpeting so much she felt like ripping it up with her fingernails. She was not in the least old. It was absurd to feel like this.

There was a payphone in the corridor. No handbag. It was in the car. What was happening to her? She asked the receptionist, could she borrow some change, and add it to the bill? As she waited for the call to go through, she watched the doorway, but allowed herself to take fleeting glances at the emerald. It looked completely perfect on her hand. The one good thing in all this absurdity.

When her own recorded voice asked her to leave a message, she was sorely tempted to yell.

'Paul, if you get this, I'm at a hotel in the middle of nowhere. Apparently someone is trying to kill me.' Why had she said that? It sounded ridiculous. 'Anyway, phone me the moment you get this. We have to talk. Here's the number.'

She read it into the phone, and hung up, greatly relieved that she was still on her own. Charles would probably not approve. In fact, she decided, it was probably better not to tell him.

'Thank you so much,' she gave the girl her most winning smile. 'I'm expecting someone to phone me here. It's very . . .' She took a business card from the stack and borrowed the desk pen to write her name on the reverse. 'Very confidential. So when my friend calls back, could you come to the conservatory and ask me to come to reception without saying why?'

159

The girl didn't understand.

'Just come for me, don't say there's a phone call. I'm in the conservatory. It's . . . a special surprise for the gentleman I'm with.'

This time the girl smiled and nodded.

'Your tea's getting cold,' Charles said. 'I thought you'd got lost.'

She took a sip. 'Oh it's not too bad.'

They'd brought shortbread with the tea, not homemade, but edible. She finished both small biscuits. Was there actually someone out there wanting to kill her? She hoped Paul would call back quickly. Or Ronni. They were both reliable. The phrase 'joined-up thinking' might have been invented to describe them. If they were here, they'd be telling her not to worry. The tea was lukewarm, but not unpleasant. She wanted to show them the ring, and tell them about the offer, tell them about all the possibilities that might lie ahead. Paul had always been interested in her heritage, in Byzantine art and architecture. She wanted them all here to recognise what was happening. By phoning, she had done the right thing, and they would come.

'Tell me, Charles, what happens next? What's the master plan?'

He was chewing his crusts.

'You said that man with the damaged face wants to kill me, but you let his friend go. So now he's roaming free. So why are we sitting here in a public place? And why are we going further and further into the depths of nowhere? I'm getting very weary of all these endless lochs and mountains. Hello? Are you hearing any of this?'

He pushed his plate away, leaned back in his chair and half turned to look at the view, as if he was trying to work out why on earth she could be tiring of it.

'Are you going to . . .?'

'Do you want your secretary back unharmed, Irene?'

'Of course.'

'Good. I just felt we might have lost sight of her for a minute. Stopped caring, as it were.'

Who the hell did he think he was?

'I haven't stopped thinking about her for a single moment,' she said.

He swung back to face her. 'What do you see when you look at me, Irene?'

'What the hell does that have to do with anything?'

He took her right hand in his left. His steady blue gaze made her uneasy. She hadn't given Dina a thought for a long time. He didn't let her hand go. He stroked the finger with the emerald ring.

He glanced at the others in the room. His voice dropped almost to a whisper. 'Let me answer for you. You see one man. I, on the other hand, when I see my sorry self reflected in this large, though not impeccably clean window, see not one man but many. I see an organised body of men. Team players, for want of a better phrase. People I trust. People who trust me. This is the way I live.'

He squeezed her hand gently and let it go. 'Our foreign friend should have phoned by now and he hasn't. I'm going to call my boss. Wait here for me, won't you? Order coffee for me. Double espresso. I won't be long.'

He stood under the dark maroon canopy at the doorway. Although it wouldn't be long before the light began to fade, some of the sky was showing blue again. He took deep breaths of the fresh salty air. How wearisome all this was becoming. It had been amusing at first, pretending to be some kind of James Bond figure, watching her varying reactions, but the fun was fast wearing thin. She was possibly the most self-absorbed, vain woman he had ever met.

If she patted her hair one more time he might scream and pull it all out of her dumb head.

He slipped a piece of mint gum into his mouth and begin to chew, avoiding the left side of his jaw which was still tender. She was right about one thing, they were going further and further into the wilderness, no nearer the foreign guy, no closer to payback time. It should be done and dusted by now. It should have ended on the roof.

He checked her mobile. Nothing. That was seriously annoying. So much depended on them phoning. No phone call opened up too many possibilities. He didn't like clutter. The scarred man and the MacLeod girl could both identify him and he believed the man actually did want to get the bitch back. If they didn't call him, the likeliest thing was that the police had caught up with them. In which case, he himself should be sensible and cut his losses. But leaving loose ends had never been his way. It made life harder, but that was the way it was. Some people tidied up after themselves, others didn't. The matter of Dan, for example – that wasn't something he'd had in mind. Once only in the past had he been compelled to tidy up in that fashion. Twice if you counted the nervous foreign guy's recent fall. And that time in Gibraltar . . . But that had been an accident, more or less.

He looked at his shirt cuffs in distaste. And two days in the same underwear. All his stuff was in a suitcase in the boot of his own car, in a city street. Swings and bloody roundabouts, he told himself. Still, no need to be gloomy. There was always the ring. If the foreign guy and the girl were out of reach, the emerald would be compensation enough for the inconvenience and waste of time. He had to admit he'd made a bit of a mistake back there, not realising quite how close to the road they were. It would have been better if he'd fallen somewhere else, where his body might have lain undiscovered for days. Oh well, not to worry.

She might not let the ring leave her finger. In which case, he supposed, the finger would have to come too. He patted the firm line of Dan's knife in its sheath in his inside pocket. He'd always looked down on weapons, but it was good to be open to new possibilities in life.

He walked across the gravel, to where he could see the loch. The waves were still the colour of lead despite the clearing sky, and probably very cold. Would Irene like to take a brief reviving stroll along the shore? They might wander down to look for little fish, down the cracked concrete ramp where an upturned boat lay, its dark blue paint peeling like aged scabs. He didn't like the sea himself. He was a terribly poor swimmer, no use to anyone who might unexpectedly slip and fall.

He spat the gum back into its wrapper and dropped it on top of a flower tub on the steps. Pinks and gypsy carnations, sadly neglected. Why did people take the trouble to plant flowers and not give them the care they needed? All it took was a little effort.

His coffee was waiting.

'Well, I've done what you wanted. I've taken advice,' he told her.

'And?' she said, not looking at him.

'And there may be one or two changes to plan.'

'So we were following a plan?'

'They're sending someone else to get Miss MacLeod back. I'm off duty.' He tried the coffee. It tasted of washing-up liquid.

She looked not altogether pleased. 'What does that mean?'

'It means we can relax,' he gave her his warmest smile. 'It means you can go home.'

She didn't look happy at all. He wasn't entirely con-
vinced by this new twist in the story himself. One secret
agent on the loose was plausible. Others lurking about the
hills waiting to leap like the deer into action was perhaps a
little less so. She was playing with the handle of a teaspoon,
pushing it back and forth on the dark-stained wood.

'Of course, I'm not completely off duty. I'm still responsible for your safety so I'll stay with you to the finish.'

This was pure mischief. Being 'responsible' was a
concept he had never been able to fathom, though he'd
pondered it more than once.

'You said he wouldn't let Dina go unless I was there.'

Shit. He'd forgotten that. 'I know, but the powers that
be have decided your safety is paramount. That's the long
and short of it. What's the matter?'

'I'd like my phone back.'

'Of course. I'm sorry. It's in the car.'

'Have they found the other one? The man you turned
loose. What if he turns up again?'

He would almost certainly have turned up by now,
Charles thought, and he was almost tempted to tell her
why, but really, maintaining the mystery was much more
jolly. An explanation could be saved for another time.

'Oh, I don't think he'll bother us again,' he said. 'Now, if
you'd care to accompany me, young lady, I think we might
take a little fresh air before we turn around. Frankly, I'd like
a hot shower, but that's not going to happen. You know, I
wasn't told much about you before I was assigned, and I
would really like to hear more. I'm not quite off duty, as I
said, but I do feel I deserve to enjoy your company before
I have to give you up.'

She agreed to the walk but wanted an overnight bag
from the car boot, as well as her handbag. 'To freshen up,'
she said.

He brought them in, and off she strode, leaving him to his own devices. He went over to the reception desk to pay. That done, he took one of the black leather tub chairs just inside the door and sat with a newspaper. Everything was the same as always. Politicians caught with other men's wives or other men. Banks making excuses. Virus outbreaks all over the place. Middle Eastern rulers being rebelled against. Church leaders telling everyone how to live without ever explaining why. People were so stupid, so determined to make their lives complicated. If only they'd learn to live simply and control themselves. But then, he mused, what would the newspapers find to print?

'Oh, excuse me.' It was the receptionist. She'd left her desk to come to him. 'Were you with the blond lady in the linen suit? In the conservatory?'

'That's right. Is there a problem?'

'Could you give her this, please?'

He read the note. The writing was large and like a child's.

'From Ronnie. Asks are you ok? Should she pass your message on to the police? Call back. Paul going crazy, use his direct line.'

He smiled, 'Do we owe you for the call?'

'Oh no, sir,' she said, a frown creasing her forehead. 'You paid for it already. I added it to the bill.'

'Of course you did.' He'd missed it. Careless, Charlie boy, careless. 'Thank you so much, Frances,' he said, leaning forward to read the name on her small rectangular gold badge. 'You've been a real help.'

'Oh no, there's no need,' she said, as he then drew out his wallet.

'I've worked in a few hotels in my time, Frances,' he said. 'I was never paid what I was worth, and I'm sure you're not either.' He closed his hand around her little plump one and the money.

165

Chapter Thirty-Four

Dina drove through Glencoe village in a state of misery. Frank's car was an automatic, which took a bit of getting used to. Frank's legs were obviously a lot longer than hers, but she'd found the right button to move the seat forward so that her feet touched the pedals. Why couldn't all cars have the same buttons? She didn't know how to get more air without making the whole inside cold. Nor did she dare suggest stopping at a phone box, although she knew the time to make the call had come and gone. *I'm not afraid of him,* she told herself. *I just don't care anymore. I don't care if Lazslo's alive or dead, I don't care about Irene, and I completely do not care how he feels or what he does. He's mad, that's all.* Eventually they would roll to a stop, and then what? *I don't care.*

When the road divided and Feliks said nothing, she took the Ballachulish road, crossing over the metal bridge, which was now pale blue, not green as she remembered it. Beneath them, Loch Leven stretched out to the right, Loch Linnhe to the left towards the sea.

She didn't look at them, she knew they were there, because they always had been: all she saw was the road ahead. The world had narrowed rather like a fatty artery, clogged by too much talk and people being vulnerable and hurt and shot, and she had, she decided, simply stopped caring about any of it.

They passed a sign giving the miles to Fort William.

'Fort William,' he said. 'What is that? Army? Navy?'

'It's just a town. A big town. We're running out of petrol.'

He didn't reply.

She slowed as they reached the outskirts. Edwardian mansions behind tall trees, wrought iron railings above century-old walls. Vacancies / No Vacancies, the signs said, and here was the one where they'd stopped often for afternoon tea. Massive chocolate eclairs, she remembered. Or had they seemed huge because she was small? On the new road now, by-passing the town centre. *Nico's Fish and Chips* was still in existence – she saw the sign on the back end of the building. But she didn't care about food.

And what are you going to do when he tells you to stop the car? Run? Get shot like Frank?

How loud the gulls were, screaming at one another as they swooped overhead. The Hospital came and went, and the new Fitness Centre, exactly and ironically opposite the graveyard.

'Pull in there,' he said suddenly.

It was a filling station. She managed to slow in time. And now, when another chance to fight or flee presented itself, she didn't scream or run. Instead, she sat where she was while he filled the tank, then did as she was bid, following him into the shop without a murmur. There was a hot drinks machine and a chill cabinet, rows of vegetables, newspapers with the usual shock horror headlines, magazines with celebrities gaining weight and losing weight and doing the stupid things they were always doing. He asked what she would like, and stood beside her at the till to pay. She didn't care whether she ate or not. She did nothing, didn't even look the cashier in the face, all the while thinking how very strange this was, that she was standing compliantly beside a madman when she

167

ought to have been screaming her head off. Somebody's syndrome. She'd heard of it.

He had her drive on until they were clear of the town. Then he told her to stop, giving her the carton of tomato soup and one of the packs of sandwiches. Her body betrayed her completely, insisting that she did care. It insisted that the warmth of tomato soup was wonderful, that garage tuna sandwiches tasted like something out of Heaven's best delicatessen. Beside her, the madman was eating a banana, taking tiny bites of it, chewing it in slow motion almost, looking out into space as if she wasn't there.

Come back, Frank, she begged. *Don't be dying like Lazslo.* If only Frank would appear, as he had in the beginning, as he had in the traffic queue. Frank the provider of milk chocolate who was bleeding somewhere back down the road. She told herself that Frank was fine. Frank was a policeman. He would be all right. He would boldly stop the next passing car. Frank had found them before and would find them again. He might even find Irene.

'What happens now? I mean, I'm happy for you to shoot anyone you feel like shooting, happy to drive all over the Highlands, but I'd like to feel there was a purpose to it, you know? Can't help it, it's just the way I am.'

The words sounded so clear in her head she almost believed she'd spoken them aloud.

I can't stand it. I cannot stand this silent banana-chewing madman any longer. I may quite probably go mad myself. Any time now. Which will be a relief. Because then I won't have to try to make sense of anything at all.

They passed through Spean Bridge and Letterfinlay, with the long dark grey stretch of Loch Lochy on their left. Since he didn't tell her to stop or change direction, she simply drove on. They were getting closer and closer to her old home and every landmark let loose a memory. They passed the line of electricity pylons with their feet dug into the hillside and arms akimbo. *Do you see that sparrow on the wire? If he puts one foot on the ground he'll be electrocuted.* Her father's old joke.

They crossed the Caledonian Canal on the swing bridge at Laggan, then passed the sign to Mandally. *'On the road to Mandalay, where the flying fishes play'.* They'd sung the ancient song together, her child soprano and his light tenor harmonising. For years she'd thought the old song really was about Mandally, and that there were flying fish there.

'Too much hard work,' everyone said. Too much diligence, too much caring for his patients. No one said anything about his personal unhappiness. How could you blame them? He'd kept it well hidden. Not one mean word about her mother.

This wasn't good for her. She forced her mind back to the present as they passed into the gloom of Glenshiel. School project, she told herself, Bonnie Prince Charlie and the Spanish being defeated by the weather. *'Good content, Donaldina. Improve your handwriting!!'* Nothing grew here but conifers, and many, she saw, had been recently felled, leaving a desolation of splinters and half trunks, as if the hillside had been bombed. At Shiel Bridge she automatically took the familiar road to the right. Over the loch on the causeway, then through Inverinate. And onwards wound the road, Eilean Donan on the left as ever, grey and grim in the failing light, with its elbows in the water. Then Kyle. Ramshackle, functional, unplanned, and ugly. She had always hated Kyle.

Onto the island they went, through Breakish, Skulamus, Harrapool. The golf club house was still the same, still looked exactly like a toilet block.

Chapter Thirty-Five

Feliks was hardly aware of the changing scenes. His thoughts drifted, debris swirling slowly in a mill pool. The day's events re-played yet seemed unreal. Why was he still here in this alien country?

If I'd been one of those secret agents in the war, with the poison capsule fixed in their mouths, I'd have been the one with the placebo. One bite and you live on.

Why did he have to believe that Boris would keep his word? Millions of people all over the planet didn't keep their promises and slept well enough. He'd been brought up to believe in keeping his word, that was the tragedy of it. He was trapped because of how his mother had brought him up. She'd been frequently in tears, yet tenaciously religious, her faithful soul proofed somehow against his father's rants and the realities of life. He'd not been able to bear it when the girl had gone into her jittery question mode, the way she'd been at the very beginning. After a minute or two he'd guessed from the small sounds beside him that she was crying.

He became aware that they were crossing a wide expanse of water. The voice in his head began again:

Talk to her. Tell her why you shot him. Explain.

She wouldn't believe it. She probably thought Frank was a big friendly bear. She'd never seen a real bear, not like the ones at home. Dangerous, flea-bitten, defecating on paths, rummaging through rubbish heaps in the darkness . . .

Tell her, the voice insisted.

'I would like to tell you why I shot him back there.'

There, that was a beginning. Perhaps not the best one possible, judging by her face.

'First, I don't trust anyone who carries a gun. All right, I know, I used it. But I shot to wound him, only to slow him down. I am a very good shot. My father taught me when I was a boy. I'm also competent with sticks and stones, and the Australian boomerang.'

Not the slightest glimmer of a smile. It was true about the boomerang. He'd been given one for Christmas when he was nine. Green and black stripes and dots on pale wood. He'd brought down pigeons for the pot. Great fun until another child managed to break a window with it.

'Also, he lied to us in the beginning about being a news reporter. That was not necessary. I am not certain an ordinary person can listen to the police communication, so I ask myself, how did he find us? In fact he keeps finding us. And if he is working for your government, which is his story now, why is he telling a mixture of lies and truth?'

'You tell me,' she said.

He hated the indifference in her voice.

'I cannot reason it all out. He makes it sound so clear. Perhaps that is why I don't trust him. He told the truth about the oil. There are massive reserves in my country waiting to be exploited. It is also true that my father wants Miss Arbanisi to come home because that will help him. Somehow she is important to him. Then I ask myself why exactly does he want her? I don't know. No one can know what his plans are. Certainly, this is all about oil. Clearly he will need foreign help to get the oil out, but he needs also to stay secure, you know? To please all who might oppose him. Then I ask, can Frank have learned about the oil from my father? Perhaps. So why not admit it? Perhaps he is working for some other party.'

171

'Why does that matter?'

'Because I think they should not know yet either. I myself am not supposed to know. Therefore, the information has been obtained covertly. Did you hear me say the name Janek?'

She nodded.

'Janek is a thoroughly bad man who works for my father. Who is of course also bad, but not in quite the same way. No one who knows anything about my country could fail to know his name. So that was another needless lie. But worst of all, Frank also mentioned Dimitar, who is my best friend in the entire world, who has a head shining like the Buddha, and cannot speak in any way whatsoever since before I was born. So that is why I shot Frank. Whoever he is, he does not mean good to us or to Miss Arbanisi.'

He wasn't sure if he was making complete sense, but it was as far as his mind would take him. It had been a long time since he'd had to think in a lengthy or logical way. A scan of his brain would, he imagined, have shown great blank spaces where connections had once been.

'No, you mustn't cry,' he said, seeing her eyes begin to fill. 'I won't let him hurt you. You do believe me?'

Why should she? Lazslo lay dying in a ditch, death and eternity were all around them and he'd demonstrated his nobility of soul by kissing her and shooting a stranger.

'What happened to Lazslo?'

'I don't know.'

'How did Frank know his name? His other name.'

'I told him.'

After a little she said, 'We're never going to find Irene, are we?'

He guessed what she was really asking, but he had no answer for that either.

172

Chapter Thirty-Six

Frank was taking stock. He'd always been fond of the little Walther. It was light and eminently concealable, but of course he'd never been shot with it before. Cautiously, he lowered his trousers and examined his thigh. Two neat quarter-inch holes, front and back. It hurt like hell, but the bullet had gone straight through the muscle and exited cleanly. It felt not unlike the shoulder wound five years back, although that had been sheer bad luck, a case of mistaken identity. Forget that, he told himself. Past memories could do more damage than bullets. The roads back there were barricaded.

Quickly he pulled off his sweater and t-shirt, wrapped the shirt tightly around the wounds, put the sweater back on. He'd been shot with his own gun, and he was thoroughly cold and wet, especially around the bum area, on a moor, with only one house in sight. No car, no phone, no wallet. Not as bad as it might be then. 'I am not being paid enough for this,' he told himself, not for the first time. No recriminations though. Time for that later. He'd never been the type to sit around getting morose.

So what happens now?

What happens is, you get out of this sodden field, and you limp along this road, trying not to weep or fall over, until you get somewhere. Or until someone stops to help you. Possibly even a police car. Which would be highly embarrassing.

There was still a job to be done. First things first.

Brenda said childbirth was worse than being shot, but he doubted it. Sometimes he wished he hadn't studied so hard at University. If he hadn't got a bloody first he'd not have been recruitment material, he'd be in the private sector, or even retired from it, sitting comfortably beside a pool somewhere, with a long cold drink in his hand, cultivating his tan.

Well, this wasn't bad luck, but it wasn't stupidity on his part either. He'd done his homework, done his best with the material he'd been given. Berisovic had no track record of violence. Short-tempered, egocentric, confrontational – yes. Violent – no. Maybe the loss of Christescu had been a turning point of some kind.

Should he have admitted knowing the name Janek, Boris Albescu's right-hand man? He'd flipped a mental coin. Sod's Law. What can go wrong, will go wrong. Find a phone. The bungalow up ahead was the obvious first move. Maybe they'd have information on the woman's kidnapper by now.

He made it to the white bungalow, rehearsing his opening speech, but there was no one around. He broke into the garage from the rear. No car, but as good if not better, a smart black Yamaha XV 950, with its key hidden in plain sight in a glass pickle jar. 'Oh careless, careless motorbike owner. I do love you,' he said aloud.

The door to the kitchen wasn't even locked. No food smells, no breakfast dishes. There was a fine selection of alcohol in another cupboard, including whisky miniatures, one of which he drank, several of which he pocketed.

Then he used the householder's own headed notepaper and pen to write a quick note, explaining and apologising for the theft of the motorbike, the whisky, a waxed jacket, and the use of the facilities, and giving a number to call for a fuller explanation and compensation.

They had a large laminated wall map in the corridor between the kitchen and the front of the house, which told him exactly where he was. Even more helpfully, there was a list of numbers beside the phone, including that of the local doctor. Oh, how he loved these noble, organised, generous people. He loved their whisky and their careless attitude to security. There were family photographs on the fridge. 'Thank you, dear Bob and Margaret,' he said, kissing two fingers and touching their smiling faces. 'I wish you and your lovely daughters the very best, wherever you may be.'

The doctor turned out to be a heavily bearded bachelor. He had not gone to bed and was not surprised to be stirred from his chair by a stranger. 'Happens a lot,' he said non-chalantly. 'Not a great many bullet wounds, though. I'll get you to hospital. Quicker than an ambulance. I'm thinking you've had a drink or two?'

Frank confessed to the whisky, and declined the trip to hospital, explaining as best he could. The doctor thought it over, then got to work with no more questions. He was a young man of strong opinions who believed among other things that all politicians were merely moving deckchairs on the Titanic. He was also staunchly opposed to soap and shampoo, he told Frank, because they were ruining the planet. Fortunately he was not opposed to antibiotics and painkillers when there was a real need. Once the wound was dealt with he offered Frank the use of his phone and went to make tea. He brought back a pair of jeans with the tea, but they were too tight around the waist to be of any use. The damaged ones would have to do. Frank drank some tea and made the call. He left the door open so that the doctor could hear if he wanted to.

'It's Frank.'

'How can I help you, Frank?'

'I need to know where my car is,' he said.

'Oh dear. Altzheimer's strikes again. You're getting old, Frank. You and that stunning wife of yours still together, by the way?'

This was said with such obvious spite that he would have hit the owner of the voice if he could have.

"I suppose you're in real need,' the voice went on, 'since you've had to call us. Shouldn't take long. This line ok?'

He promised it was. 'And check if there's something for me.'

There was a brief interval of clicking. He could hear other voices in the background, the noise of a drawer being shut, faint laughter. 'I can give you that right now,' the voice said. 'We think your mystery man is called Charles Bedlay, or Charles De Bono, or Carl Brereton. No criminal record. Interesting, that, in view of all the name changes. D'you have a fax there?'

'Just tell me.'

'Well, salient facts are, born London, schooled locally. Father deceased, mother extant in London, two siblings of no apparent interest to us or anyone, in Canada. No further education, various unimportant jobs, then progress into charity fundraiser posts and religious counselling services. That's about it.'

'Thanks for nothing,' he said.

'Oh, don't be grumpy, Frank. It doesn't suit you. We're still digging. Stay there and I'll call back as soon as.'

Before very long the phone rang again. The signal was loud and clear, they told him. His car was stationary. He noted the co-ordinates. This encouraged him greatly. Of course there was the possibility that Berisovic and his companion had found another vehicle or were travelling on foot, but he liked to think that they'd merely stopped for the night.

The young doctor again suggested hospital, but Frank

176

declined. Then he offered a bed, which Frank accepted. Exactly how much pain relief had the doctor given him? He certainly wasn't fit to ride a bike in darkness.

'You wouldn't have an Ordnance Survey map I could borrow?' he said. They could be in a hotel, or an empty cowshed. They could be with aliens in a flying saucer for all he knew, but it was more likely they were simply sleeping in a lay-by. The map was produced. He circled the spot. It was always good to know where you were going even if you didn't know what was waiting for you there.

He checked for anxiety and oddly it wasn't there. The medication probably.

As soon as his head went down on the pillow, he began to slip away off into a strangely contented darkness. One thing would lead to another. Cristescu had died with the tracker from Miss Arbanisi's car in his jacket pocket, for reasons unknown, but find Berisovic and he'd surely be a step closer to finding her. Pain woke him before five. He swallowed two of the capsules beside the bed before getting up. He got dressed without washing.

The doctor, in pyjamas, came down the stairs as Frank opened the front door. It looked like being a sunny day.

'Let me change the dressing.'

Frank shook his head.

'At least you should eat something. I wish you wouldn't do this,'

'I wish I didn't have to. The phone didn't ring through the night, did it?'

'No. Look, you should have something in your stomach . . .'

'I'll be fine.'

'In my professional opinion, you're an idiot,' the young man scratched his head. 'And you're breaking the law, on that thing without a helmet.'

'Believe me, I break the law all the time.' Frank got astride the bike, not without crying out. The pain went right through him, right to his teeth and beyond.

'Don't overdo those pills I gave you. And don't mix them with anything. Especially alcohol. I don't want to be struck off.'

'No problem.'

'The fact is, I don't want to read about you in tomorrow's paper.'

'Don't worry,' Frank called back, 'It wouldn't be in the newspaper.'

Still, he rode with care. The cold air on his face helped. It seemed like a very long time since he'd tailed the two men from the airport to their rustic retreat, and to the Arbanisi woman's flat the following morning. His bosses hadn't anticipated trouble. 'He's the President's son, estranged, he's been off the grid for years.' Where? They didn't know. Apparently. Sometimes things were kept from people at various levels. Insurance, they called it. 'We don't think he'll go looking for trouble, and the other one's a lightweight, a civil servant of some kind.' It looked like an odd pairing, a very strange choice for an undercover diplomatic mission – a son, out of favour, and a desk man, with no one along to protect them. He'd pointed this out, carefully, on more than one occasion, to more than one recipient, to cover himself by having it on record in more than one person's files, but nobody had seemed bothered. So there it was, and there it would be, on record. A little insurance of his own. His misgivings and their decision to proceed, all waiting to be pointed out after the dust settled.

He'd always been cautious, even when there was no double dealing involved. Bless their little slipper'd feet, they ought to have dug for more salient (their word) details from the very start, in wider, deeper circles. Bedlay or

Bono or whatever his name was, nobody had anticipated him at all. Some of them were first-rate, but some weren't so clever as they thought they were. Or maybe it was a lack of motivation. It was too much like a game for some of the young ones. They didn't have responsibilities and bills to pay like his generation. He stopped on the crest of a hill, straightened the leg, circled his foot and relaxed it again. It felt a bit easier.

Chapter Thirty-Seven

Charles let the car window down a fraction. It looked as if it was going to be a bright morning, from what he could see of the sky through the branches, though the air was cold. Condensation on the windows. He shivered. He was thirsty and hungry, but there was nothing to be done about that right away. He glanced in the mirror. Huddled in the back seat, Irene was still sleeping beneath her blanket, which struck him as little short of astonishing. Unless she'd died of shock. He listened very carefully, and was relieved to hear slight snoring sounds.

'You look wonderful,' he'd told her, when she came back from her prettifying session. 'God, how do you do it?' he'd added, after a suitable pause. 'You're still gorgeous, after all I've put you through.'

It worked every time. The eyes softened, the head went just a fraction to one side, the hand went briefly to the hair. It was hilarious. She didn't object to the cancellation of their walk along the shoreline, and they were several minutes on the road before it dawned on her that they were going north, not south. He'd thought for a moment or two, and when no plausible explanation came to mind, he'd decided to stop being a secret agent. It had been fun, but he was tired of it. She'd not been best pleased, but the first little flurries of disbelief, indignation, and anger had melted like snow in summer after a few hard slaps. Her collapse was so easy, it took

180

him by surprise. No need for the knife. He'd taken the emerald ring off her finger without a cheep of protest. Who'd have thought?

He got out to relieve himself, and when he turned round, she was awake. The inrush of cold air or the noise of the car door opening, he supposed. She wasn't quite so lovely now. To be fair, he recalled, he'd had to slap her about quite a bit before she saw sense.

'Sleep ok?' he said, opening the passenger door.

No answer. What was wrong with her? Where had the feistiness gone? If she stayed as submissive as this to the bitter end, it would be a bit of a let-down.

'You brought this on yourself, Irene,' he reminded her. 'I trusted you, but you didn't trust me. Now see where it's got you.'

'Please . . .'

'Please what, my love? Please don't hurt you? I'm not going to hurt you. I had to hurt you a little last night because you were being silly. But you're not being silly anymore, are you?'

She gave a tiny shake of the head.

'Good girl. You see, I like to keep things simple. Life is meant to be simple, don't you think? I wanted your nice stuff, but people kept getting in the way, and making everything confused, which just isn't right. Even your stupid cat got under my feet. This is better, isn't it? I wanted the ring, you gave me the ring. That makes me happy. And when Dina called last night, you had a little chat and she was happy too. And today we're going to meet her and the foreign guy, and everybody's going to be very happy. Well, not for very long, but some happiness in this life is better than none at all. God, I'm hungry. Are you hungry?'

Her eyes told him nothing at all.

'Well, that's good. That's a simple thing,' he looked at his watch. 'We'll get out of this forest and find something to eat.'

He had no idea what would happen next, but in his heart he knew it would be fine. The police might be around sooner or later, thanks to her foolish phone call at the hotel, which might make things merry. Once they were on the main road he'd rehearse some options. He'd always liked lists, and Mind Maps even more, where you could colour in circles and join them with curly or straight lines. He'd had a gold felt tip pen once, and a silver one, just for drawing lines. Where had they gone? Making lists was fun, but sometimes it was even more fun just to take what life gave you. Like Irene making her phone call and that fat dimwit of a receptionist dropping the message in his lap.

Essentially, life was very much like driving. If you looked too far ahead all the time, you'd lose sight of the car in front, when it was that one that caused the danger. In just the same way, if you thought too much about the future, things got so complex you couldn't live today. Of course you had to keep half an eye on the car behind, particularly if it was a police car, but not too much. Just half an eye. He never held grudges. He could still remember that prefect, Trevor, who'd reported him for stealing way back in his short trouser days. A word or two in his ear, and he'd been eager to retract his accusation. They'd got on well after that, with a constant supply of chocolate biscuits, Trevor's father being the manager of a biscuit factory. Happy days.

He reversed the car carefully down the track. It was narrow and the ruts were deep and the pine branches threatened to scratch the paintwork. 'Put your seat belt on, my love,' he reminded her. Money did grow on trees, no matter what anyone said. He didn't want to take it from

182

people, but it was just so easy. He glanced at her in the mirror. Possibly her collapse wasn't so surprising. She lived in a bubble of vanity. One prick and she deflated. Nobody loved her anymore. He tried to imagine what that might feel like.

Chapter Thirty-Eight

Feliks woke soon after dawn. There were no curtains in the attic bedroom. The window, set into the sloping roof, allowed no view of his surroundings, but the sky was clear. And the room was warm. She had switched on the heating the night before and turned it on full. He pulled the covers over his head and tried unsuccessfully to get back to sleep.

He had slept naked. His underpants, socks and trousers on the radiator had thankfully dried enough to be wearable. He found his shirt and jacket next to the radiator in the bathroom on a wooden frame, very like the one from his childhood. He was reminded of how his mother had hung clothes over it in front of the stove, on winter mornings warming them item by item before he put them on. The shirt was ok but the jacket was still completely sodden. He turned it outside in and draped it back over the rail. His shoes beneath were still wet too.

There were a few pairs of black rubber boots in the porch at the rear of the house, but none big enough for him. He took off the socks. Easier to go barefoot.

He knew already that the front of the small house was separated from the road by a low stone wall, with no garden to speak of. At the back was a steep garden accessed by a flight of five stone steps. He liked that. It made the house seem to sit comfortably in its space as one might sit in an armchair. There were beds edged with stones, growing nothing but weeds, the paths between a mixture of bare earth, moss and broken tarred surfacing. He climbed over a low fence into a steeper grassy field. The grass was wet, misted with dew. Sheep marked with blue dye on their heavy fleeces stopped feeding to stare at him and bolted as he came closer. He stepped carefully to avoid their droppings. How fat and healthy-looking these animals were. Life was easy when you were too dumb to know there was a future, grew your own clothes and could chew your bed the whole day long.

He scanned the long sweep of the bay. No shops at all. She'd said there was nothing to eat in her house, so they'd paused the previous evening at a supermarket, a large one, right beside the water. She'd gone to pay for the ticket. The car park was busy. Vans, a tour bus. A surprising number of small children running about freely with no parents around. Houses behind tall bushes on the other side of the road. Lots of traffic. He heard foreign voices. Hungarian he thought. He knew some Hungarian. The man was on his mobile, telling someone – a son or daughter – what time to come back, asking what they would eat, and what they wouldn't. His wife was checking a map.

When he hung up, Feliks got out of the car.

'Excuse me, are you from Hungary?' he asked in Hungarian.

Smiles of pleasure. Where was he from? What was he doing here?

'I'm working,' he said, 'It's good money. You're on holiday? The weather's not so good for a holiday. Look, it's cheek of me to ask, but could I make a quick call from your phone? I'll pay you for it. It's just a local call. Mine's dead. Here's my girlfriend coming. It's for her, in fact. She needs to make a call. You can see how miserable she is.'

They didn't need to look twice to see he was telling the

185

truth. And of course he could make a call. No question of payment. No, don't be ridiculous.

They passed the phone to Dina.

'Call Irene,' he told her.

She dialled the number.

So, had he been in the country long? What did he think of it? They were camping, with their son and daughter. The people were friendly but the English food was terrible.

Absolutely, he agreed. He missed goulash and proper chicken soup. And Hortobagyi pancakes. There was a place in Budapest in a back street near the castle, he said, where they did wonderful pancakes, and the best peach palinka. Ah, yes, they thought they knew it. (Interesting, since he'd just made it up.) The place with the violinist who always played just slightly out of tune? Yes, he remembered that one. Just as well the tourists hadn't found it yet or the prices would shoot through the roof.

'Irene? Where are you? Are you all right?' Dina's voice interrupted the exchange of happy memories.

Feliks couldn't hear what Irene was saying. 'Yes, on the island,' Dina said. There was much more from Irene, to which Dina said, 'Yes, of course.' Then, 'Park anywhere in the town square. It's not far. That's right. You're sure he's gone?'

She handed the phone back to the woman, who talked to her in Hungarian.

'She won't understand you. She's Scottish,' he told them. 'She lives here.'

'Lucky man,' the husband said, laughing. 'Does she have a job too?'

'Of course. Rich and beautiful. What more does a man need?'

'Teenage children,' the woman offered. Laughter and smiles all round. Perhaps we'll see you again. Have a great holiday. Thank you so much. Yes, and take care on the roads. They don't give you much space here. So, just like home really.

'Well? Tell me,' he said, when they'd gone.

'It was Irene. She says she's all right. She says she got rid of him.'

'Really?'

'She said she told him one of the tyres felt soft, and he got out and she drove away without him. She wants to meet us tomorrow. You, I mean. She wants to meet you. I suggested a place.'

'Did she sound like herself?'

'She sounded tired, but she said she's completely ok. She's going to find a hotel and meet us tomorrow.'

He let her believe it, though he didn't. There were too many pieces missing, and he was certain a man like that wouldn't be duped so easily. To persuade Dina otherwise right now seemed too cruel, like crushing a butterfly. She would work it out herself, given time. If they had time.

'Why will she not come to your house?'

She sighed. 'That would have been better. I'll phone her again when we get there. I've got tins, but as I said, there's no fresh food. What would you like?' she said. 'Are you allowed to drink wine? Being a priest, I mean.'

She had cooked pasta with a meat sauce. It was ready-made, and quick to heat. Then chocolate pastries, eclairs she called them. Cheese and biscuits, and a large bunch of red grapes, to have something healthy, she said. The pastries were good, but the grapes were very small and not particularly sweet. The wine was Italian. It went to his head very quickly which was intriguing considering how much alcohol he'd once been able to down without much effect.

She had tried calling Irene again, but without success. Still believing that Irene was safe, she was cheerful, more

187

so as the evening, and the wine, went on. Of course, she was in her own safe place. And of course, many momentous things were not mentioned. It seemed her mind had compartments. The burglars, the fall from the tower, whether Lazslo was alive or dead, what had become of Frank, and the imminent possibility of being arrested had all apparently been assigned separate drawers in her memory, with the drawers pushed shut. And the kiss that so easily surfaced in his mind, had that disappeared from hers? They had sat in separate chairs on either side of the fire. The fire, he guessed, was for emotional comfort. The central heating had warmed the place up very quickly but the fire kept her occupied; watching the logs, moving and adjusting them. Her face relaxed, and she was pleased with herself when she had the wood burning just as she wanted.

Her talk was mostly of her childhood and her grandparents, to whom the small house had belonged. About her parents she said less. Her father was dead, he learned, and her mother lived with a man in the south of Spain, but whether that had happened before or after the father's death, he was not sure. He let her do most of the talking, in part because it was in fact interesting, but more because unlike her he couldn't compartmentalise his mind. He wasn't sure how much he could say about anything without slipping up and destroying her present happiness. When it was quite late she showed him the spare bed and went to her own.

He'd gone back down to the sitting room, sitting there till the last embers turned black. Then he'd stepped out into the narrow front garden and the salted air. The night had become windy and he turned up his collar. But it was not cold, he thought, not yet. The winters here might be bad, so close to the ocean. But the house was made of stone, well-made, to withstand bad winters. He wondered how old it was. The wooden gate was rough beneath his fingers. It needed sanding and its hinges oiled.

There were no street lights. Nor was there any sand on the shore beneath his feet, only shingle, then seaweed in waxy clumps, like strips of black rubber. There were no sounds except the rush and fall of the water, and the warm coursing wind. He stopped short of the water's edge, took Frank's gun from his pocket and flung it as far as he could into the waves.

Death is not an accident, but God's doing. He could hear Father Konstantin's voice. *We know that we will die, though we pretend that we will not.*

The last time he'd tried to die he'd been drunk.

Now here he was, not drunk but not quite sober either.

He looked back at the small house. No lights. He hoped she was sleeping peacefully. He himself was entirely unconvinced that the Arbanisi woman had managed to free herself from the suited man. It was far too neat.

There wasn't much of a moon. It curved like a backward c, which meant a waxing moon. The clouds had cleared, whirled away by the night wind and the sky was cluttered with a billion useless stars. What reason was there to feel angry if Lazslo was dead, to feel ashamed of his own incompetence, or guilty over his attack on Frank? If men were all mere collections of atoms, it was completely irrational. Anger, shame, hope – they were all without meaning.

The waves were loud. The weight of water sucked back, poured forward, sucked and fell, over and over. The salt air filled his lungs. He'd never been this close to the sea, to any sea. The rivers they'd fished in at home were cold in winter, but not bottomless like this. In hot weather, even the smallest boys would swing over the pools and jump in for fun. This water would never be warm.

Not that he'd ever jumped in much. Boris had tried every method known to man to make him into a swimmer, and every emotion, from reassurance to red-faced rage, but Feliks had never trusted water, not shallow, clear, flowing rivers, not even the most tranquil of ponds, because he'd already learned from his illustrated Creatures of the World about flesh-eating fish, and guessed there were things other than tench, zander and carp dwelling deep in the water, alien creatures biding their time, hiding in the mud and mayfly larvae, looking, he imagined, a bit like lampreys but with tiny vicious teeth ready to fasten onto any pale intruding foot. In other words, he'd been a coward.

Three-legged chicken dog.

A house with a banana tree.

Death is God's doing.

He walked forward, over a final thin strip of sand. The water began to seep into his shoes. The beach sloped a little more steeply. Another couple of steps and he was in. He zipped up his jacket, reflecting as he did so how ridiculous, how pointless this was. And now he was in up to his knees. The water was in fact far colder than he'd anticipated. His trousers clung most unpleasantly to his legs, but after a few moments he could barely feel them. The outgoing rush sucked him almost off his feet. He managed to right himself. The next incoming wave hit him across the waist. His legs were now completely without sensation . . .

Someone screamed. He tried to turn, struggled to stay upright. There was a commotion in the water behind him. On heavy feet, legs that refused to move, he lurched towards the screaming, splashing shape, caught at it with freezing hands, lost her, caught her, pulled her close. Braced together against the sea, they'd stood upright, then swaying, staggering, they'd stumbled towards the shore.

He didn't smell good. Even out here on the hillside with the morning breeze blowing over him, he was pretty rank, especially around the folds. Salt water and stale sweat. A bad combination. There hadn't been enough hot water the night before for two baths, and he'd insisted on her having one. As soon as there was any hot water this morning, he would need to bathe. Fortunately there was no one here to sniff at him. Not a soul in sight. He wanted to stop time. He wanted to stay here forever.

Chapter Thirty-Nine

Dina pulled herself up in the bed, until she was half sitting. Her grandparents' bed, albeit with a new mattress and new white linen. The room was exactly as she'd abandoned it months before. The wallpaper was partly stripped off – pale yellow roses and curling leaves in a green that no natural plant could ever achieve. The old Axminster was gone, leaving bare the floorboards which she fully intended to strip and reseal. On the left of the door frame, several patches of paint showed where she'd tried possible colours. She'd decided on warm shades, since the room faced north. Fowler Pink, and Book Room Red. Then she'd turned against these, worrying that they'd make the room smaller. Pinks became more intense. So on the other side she'd tried Babouche and Citron. Irene was fond of Babouche. But making decisions was hard, and in any case, to know what was right she'd have to strip the floorboards first, so the tester pots still sat there, beside strips of old wallpaper in large white bin bags, a mood board with hardly anything on it, and a little row of Diet Coke cans that had never made it to the bin. Dust sheets covered the old-fashioned bureau and chair. They weren't valuable. Should they be stripped or painted or thrown out?

'Well, Donaldina, what next?' she said aloud.

The evening before, they'd completely ignored the possibility that there would be a 'next'. Her head hurt a little now. Not surprising, considering they'd finished the bottle between them. He'd explained that he wasn't actually a priest, but that priests weren't forbidden alcohol anyway. They'd eaten lasagne and garlic bread, which he'd said he liked. They'd talked about many things; her attempts to find a career, their very different childhoods, and the house, which she'd inherited from her grandfather. He'd been taken aback by the fact that there was a house key in a tin beneath the log pile.

'If it is so safe here, why do you live in the city?'

'There's no jobs.'

'You could make money from this, I think. People would pay to come here.'

'I can't,' she told him. 'It's in the terms of the will. I can't sell the house or let it out until I'm thirty-five. The land's different. That's let to a crofter for grazing, so I get some money from that, which helps.'

'Why did your grandfather do this?'

'He wanted to keep it in the family. My Dad was the younger son, his brother died when he was just a baby, and though there's cousins, they're in England. I was the only grandchild. I think Grampa imagined I'd have children by the time I was thirty-five, and I'd want them to have the house.'

He'd nodded, as if he agreed with the old man.

She wondered what they would have made of each other. She was awfully glad he wasn't a priest. He was a good listener, so he probably would have done that well as a priest, but she was awfully glad he wasn't.

'My mother's still alive, but they never warmed to her. She lives in Spain,' she added. As if he'd want to know. She and Dad had never divorced, so she'd expected to inherit something from Grampa too. How furious she'd been. The sale of the family home after Dad's death hadn't been enough for them.

She herself had been annoyed at first at the terms of Grampa's will, because holiday lets were so lucrative. Even with the price of fuel rising there were plenty of people keen to travel from the south to get fresh air and unspoiled countryside. But she'd forgiven the old man once she worked it out. She'd loved him so much, and Gran even more, what she could remember of her: pure white hair, and painting together on the kitchen table, with never ever a word about the mess, and perfectly shaped pancakes with raspberry jam from the garden. She'd been a greedy little child, she thought, always impatient for more.

She'd not spoken about her father, that was too deep, but told him how she'd tried nursing and waitressing and how she'd finally got the job with Arbanisi Design. He hadn't said anything about Irene, and she hadn't either. They talked about his country, about the forests and beavers, bank voles, and bears, about how you could forage for food when it was rationed or hard to get from the city. He'd been very hungry as a student, and very proud, he said, refusing help from his father because by then he'd decided he hated his politics.

'Were you an anarchist?' she had asked, feeling rather knowledgeable.

'That would depend on your definition.'

'My friend Ronni used to be one. She said it was because her father worked for the CIA.'

'Impressive. Did she tell you what she did?'

'Not in any detail. But she never goes home.'

'We never thought of ourselves as anarchists,' he said. 'We thought we were pursuing democracy. I've always thought that anarchists had some good ideas, like respecting the individual, and wanting each man to find his own cultural identity. But most people like being governed. There are too many vested interests. People who have the tiniest amount of power,' he squeezed his thumb and forefinger together, 'naturally they want things to stay as they are.'

She thought of ward sisters and consultants she'd encountered.

'I think I'd be good with some power. I just don't know how to go about getting it,' she said.

He'd smiled at that. She wasn't sure if he was laughing at her or agreeing.

'Does she paint, your friend Ronni?'

'No, she takes photographs. Why?'

'I wondered if these were her work.'

'These were Granny's.'

'They are very good, I think.'

She thought so too. Whatever else she changed in the house, the paintings would stay.

She'd gone to bed, leaving him downstairs, but she hadn't been able to get to sleep, thinking thoughts that were not exactly the kind of thoughts one ought to think in a Free Presbyterian bed. She remembered his scars and the strong muscles of his shoulders. The kiss was kind of impossible to forget. Why had he kissed her? That was the important thing. Had he been kissing *her*, or would anyone have done? Some women would have asked right out, 'what was that for?'

She'd heard the sound of music on the radio. It played for some time, then went off. After a long time, she heard the front door being opened, so she got up to see where he was going.

The water had been far colder, the pull of the current more vicious, the shelving of the beach more immediate than she ever remembered them being in childhood, She'd panicked, realising too late that instead of rescuing him she was in trouble herself. But afterwards, so little had been said. A few words each. As if nothing momentous had happened. As if he hadn't been trying to drown himself at all . . .

'What happens to me?' she had wanted to scream at him. 'If you die, what happens to me?'

She had been furious. She was still furious. And now here it was, absurdly, the morning after the night before. There would have to be breakfast, she supposed. She hadn't shopped for breakfast, hadn't thought as far ahead as breakfast. There would be porridge, if the dried milk was all right, or tinned custard, and baked beans. Or desiccated coconut. With tomato sauce if she ran hot water over the disgusting glued-on bits and got the top off.

She lifted a corner of the curtain and looked out. The water was shimmering in the dawn light, serene and innocent. Damn him. Damn him and his stupid walk into the loch. Her sheepskin slippers were at the bottom of it, or possibly floating towards Greenland. If they had a boat they could sail away. A modern day Flora and Charlie. She tried to visualise herself rowing vigorously in a tartan shawl. She pictured herself pushing him overboard.

From his perch on the hill Feliks saw lights go on in the house. If she looked out of the small kitchen window she would see him. He wanted her to see him and wave, lift the teapot, call him down to breakfast. They could grow raspberries as her grandmother had. Not plums. She had said it was too cold for plums. A bread roll with jam. Or a banana. One could buy bananas very easily. There was no need to have an actual tree.

Are you insane? Nothing has been solved. Nothing has changed. Who do you think you are?

Just myself. Just who I have always been. More wrong than right. More sinning than sinned against. A three-legged chicken dog.

He took one final look at the long curve of the bay, the low hills, and out to the faint horizon, then stood, brushing damp grass from his trousers. Several metres to his left, there was an elderly man watching him from the road. Feliks raised a hand. The man lifted his stick to acknowledge him and walked on in the direction of the house. There was a dog too, black with white. It barked, and was reprimanded.

Dina was in the kitchen. He didn't think she'd showered. Her hair was unbrushed, and there were faint lines on her face where she'd been lying on creases in the bedding, but she looked as if she'd slept well.

'I'm just boiling the kettle. I thought you were still asleep,' she said. She sounded as if she was annoyed at something

'The sun called to me. The room has no curtains. But it is all right . . .'

The doorbell interrupted him.

'I think it is a man with a stick,' he said. He followed her to the hall but stayed out of sight. He understood nothing of the conversation, except that it seemed amicable. The man spoke more slowly than Dina, in the way of the old. There were, he thought, questions and answers, and possibly she was talking to the dog as well, because her voice became the kind of voice people use when talking to animals. The whole thing seemed to him to go on for a very long time.

At last the door was closed.

'My neighbour,' she explained. 'He saw our lights last night, but he didn't recognise the car. So he came to see who it was, and he brought bread, milk and eggs,' she held up a bag, 'in case it really was me and I didn't have breakfast.'

'You have good neighbours.'

'Nosey neighbours, you mean. No, that's not fair. He's

a good soul. He knew Grampa. I'm not sure he approves of me altogether.'

'Is that the same language?' He pointed to a framed text beside the window. 'What does it say?'

She read out the lines.

'Bheir am peacadh sinn sios do uisgeachan dobhain.
Ach bheir gras sinn sabhailte gur tir.'

He wanted to know what the words meant, but she didn't translate it. 'Let's eat,' she said, going towards the kitchen. 'It looks like it's going to be a fine day. That's Scotland for you.'

He followed. She looked very sweet in her denim trousers and long bedraggled sweater. Her ankles were endearing. So small. His hand would go completely around them.

'They say we can get all four seasons in one day, that's why climbers get into trouble so often, the ones that don't know the country. Boiled or fried?'

She meant the eggs. He said he would be happy with either.

'They go up into the mountains dressed for summer, just shorts and t-shirts, and the weather changes . . .'

In his imagination he went forward, turned her round and kissed her. The good neighbour's bag seemed to read his mind and disapprove. It fell off the edge of the table, landing with a dull thud on the stone floor.

Chapter Forty

Frank dismounted from the bike, stretched his arms and his back, and tried a few tentative steps. Not great. Ignoring previous advice he swallowed a couple of the smaller pills. Doctors were always over-cautious. From up here he could see his own car, parked in front of the small cottage, but he resisted temptation. There weren't any lights on in the house yet. Some of the curtains were closed. He was pretty sure Berisovic and the girl were inside. Where else could they reasonably be? Not that reasonableness had played much of a part in what had been going on so far. This reunion was going to be tricky, especially in the opening minutes.

How would they feel about seeing him again? Hostile? Repentant? The problem was still the same. He didn't know exactly what had prompted Berisovic to shoot him in the first place, so he had no sure way of knowing what approach to take now. He was hungry. He'd been foolish not to have eaten.

Movement on the slope behind the house caught his eye. Berisovic? The shape and height were right. What was he doing out in plain sight? Inviting disaster. Had something major happened, something that had changed the whole game? Was the Countess with them? And the man de Bono or Bedlay, had something bad happened to him? He did hope so.

He watched Berisovic do nothing for a long time. A man

in a cloth cap with a black and white collie dog exited one of the nearer houses, and walked slowly down his gravel track. Berisovic stood up, as if he'd seen the old man too. At any rate he began to make his way back to the garden and into the house.

Frank waited until the elderly gent came back along the road and began climbing his own track, then he freewheeled slowly down. He wasn't, he realised, feeling his usual chirpy self. Shock, pain and blood loss and the side effects of good painkillers – it was always the same. Well, too bad, he told himself. If you want it over and done with, you have to do it. If you want extra money, you have to take risks. If you want to be back in your own armchair with the door locked and Brenda and the kids upstairs asleep, curtains drawn against the big bad world, you have to fight for it. At least this time he would be prepared to dodge the bullet.

Chapter Forty-One

Dina salvaged enough eggs to scramble, and had just put a plate of toast on the table when the front door bell rang again. She sighed.

'That might be Mrs McKinnon, she's the next up the hill.'

This time Feliks went into the sitting room and drew two inches of the curtain aside. His heart sank. He considered the man standing on the path. He went through to the tiny hallway, unbolted the door, and opened it a fraction.

'Where's Miss MacLeod? Is she here?' the man said.

'How did you find us?'

'I'll tell you, but not on the doorstep.'

Feliks began to shut the door, but Frank lodged his foot in the space. 'Please. I need your help.'

'It is her house. She will decide.'

'All right.'

At once Frank withdrew his foot, to Feliks's surprise. He'd only said that about the house because he didn't know what else to say.

'Let him in.' Dina was right there in the hall behind him. 'Let him come in. We may as well hear what he has to say. We don't need to believe it.'

'Don't say anything about Miss Arbanisi,' Feliks said.

'Why not?'

Why not indeed? It was only a gut feeling, and hadn't he decided not to trust his guts again? 'Just listen carefully,

201

and think about what he says.' He wanted to tell her not to talk about anything, but stopped himself. He had no right to order her about.

Back in the front room, Dina opened the curtains wide, flooding it with light. He watched Frank lower himself carefully into an armchair. No mention was made of the leg, though he was obviously in pain. Perhaps he liked being the noble hero. He did grunt as he leaned over to the fireplace to pick up the wine bottle they'd shared the night before, examining the label with pursed lips. Wait, Feliks told himself, pushing down the anger that was mounting in his stomach. Wait and see.

'Is the Countess here with you?'

'No. It's just us,' Dina said.

'That's a pity,' Frank said, placing the wine bottle back on the floor.

'We want to apologise about the car,' she was now telling Frank, 'but we haven't damaged it at all.'

'Do you have anything to eat?' Frank interrupted her.

'Toast? I've made some eggs.'

Don't help him, don't be so nice, Feliks begged her silently.

'Toast would be excellent,' Frank said.

She was back in moments with a plate. My toast, Feliks thought. And my mug of tea also.

'Most of our mutual problems,' Frank began, 'at least in the last forty-eight hours, have been caused by this man who calls himself Charles de Bono. Do you know where he is?'

'No,' Feliks answered for them both. He felt Frank's eyes on him, and tried to look like someone intent on being helpful.

The tea was gulped down and the toast eaten very rapidly.

'It's rather early in the morning for harsh reality,' Frank said, 'but we may as well begin. The facts seem to be these. He and his accomplice broke into Miss Arbanisi's home, intent on her antique collection, and were surprised by you, Dina. Some minutes later, hoping to speak to Miss Arbanisi, you and your colleague Mr Cristescu arrived. I was right behind you, and I parked nearby. I was there, as I told you before, to make sure that that nothing prevented your meeting with the Countess. We all know what happened next.'

'Do we?' Feliks asked.

'What matters now,' Frank ignored the question, 'is that we all work together to make things right. As matters stand, we have several advantages.'

Feliks rose to his feet. 'Perhaps you will allow us to finish breakfast while you tell us about them. Dina, you could make fresh tea, yes?'

'Of course,' she said. 'I left the boiler on. There should be loads of water. We can all have showers.'

Now she was being absurd, he thought.

'Perhaps later, thank you. I'm fine just now,' Frank said.

'Would you like some eggs? There isn't any bacon . . .'

'No, I'm not a great one for bacon anyway,' Frank told her. 'More toast would be welcome.'

Feliks stared out of the window. There was a black motorbike against the wall. The absurdity of the whole situation was only increasing moment by moment. They were dancing round one another, like ballet dancers on the edge of a precipice. What was the phrase, the elephants in the room?

'One thing has puzzled me, Frank,' he asked as they followed Dina to the kitchen. 'How do you keep finding us?'

Frank sat on the one chair with a cushion. 'Simple technology. Your hired car had a tracker in it. Mine has one too. Most unfortunately, Miss Arbanisi's has stopped functioning.'

'Then how are you going to find her?'

His question went unanswered.

'Miss MacLeod, Dina, am I correct about what happened in the flat?'

Dina nodded. 'You might not want this. It's stone cold.' She pointed to the scrambled egg.

'I'll finish it. We must not waste good fresh eggs.' Feliks sat down at the table and took up his fork. 'Is there perhaps salt?'

She brought salt and pepper from a cupboard. 'Shake hard. It might be damp,' she said.

He watched her inserting more bread into the toaster. A pot of red jam was opened and put down on the table. He looked at the salt pot, then at Frank's temple, measuring the distance.

'Tell me, how exactly did De Bono's partner get stabbed?' Frank asked.

Kafka would have relished this, Feliks thought. Eggs and toast. Salt, murder and strawberry jam. It was rather like being inside one of his stories. Or making Prince Hamlet chew gum while he talked to the ghost, or hold a hamburger in one hand and the dead man's skull in the other.

'Lazslo stabbed him in self-defence,' he said. 'Miss MacLeod was not in the room, so she cannot bear me out. To be honest I do not know if it was Lazslo's knife or his. It was left behind.'

'Do you still have my gun?'

'I'm sorry. I gave it to the ocean.'

'That's a pity. It deserved better.' Frank turned to Dina, 'The police had several theories initially, including one that had you as an accomplice, or a murderer.'

204

'Who was murdered?' Feliks asked.

'De Bono's partner.' Frank seemed puzzled at having to explain.

'We thought he would live. She had called for help, and Lazslo said the wound . . .'

'It wasn't me,' protested Dina.

'He knows that,' Feliks said firmly. 'Everyone knows that. You were in the other room.'

He was surprised the man had died.

'Is Lazslo dead too?'

'Yes, I'm sorry.'

'Was it an accident?'

Dina put more toast on the table between them.

'I don't know.'

With Lazslo gone, he was next in line. He would be blamed for the fat man's death. He waited for Frank to point this out, but Frank merely stirred his tea. He didn't look good, and his movements were all careful. Feliks wondered where he had spent the night, and how the wound had been dealt with, then hardened his heart. The man was not to be trusted, no matter how much pain he was in. Lazslo had been barely alive at the roadside. Frank had given them false hope.

'What are the advantages you spoke of?' he asked.

'Well, we have my car.'

'And a motorbike.'

'Which we mustn't use anymore, since it's not mine. But we have back-up if we need it, and an excellent place to start from.'

'What does that mean?' Feliks asked.

'Here, of course. Your telephone, Miss MacLeod. And Miss Arbanisi's mobile number. You have called her, Miss MacLeod, haven't you?'

Dina bit her lip, looked at the floor.

'Oh, grow up, Feliks, why don't you?' Frank turned on him. 'You're not going to sit there and let her perjure herself again, are you? Listen, my children, I already have the number. I have her office number, her home number, her email, her shoe size and the same information for every member of the firm. I need you because the main advantage we have is that she and De Bono don't know me. That's why I need you to call her now. You still don't trust me, do you? How can I convince you?' He rubbed his forehead. 'One easy way would be for me to make a phone call, and sit here eating this very nice toast and jam until Special Branch arrive and arrest you both.'

'She hasn't done anything.'

'Of course she has. Obstructing the course of justice, car theft, accomplice in the wounding of an officer of the Crown, the list goes on.'

'All right,' Feliks said. 'Miss Arbanisi is on her own. She got away from De Bono. She's going to meet us at twelve o'clock.'

'Here?'

'In the town centre.'

'But we were thinking here would be better. We were going to phone her again anyway,' Dina said. Her voice sank to a whisper.

'Thank you,' Frank said. He looked at his watch, then rose slowly from the table with a last corner of toast in one hand. 'Let's keep things as they are. I want back-up on this from now on, and we're far too exposed here. One road, open country, not so good. It's better to meet somewhere public. I take it that's my car key. And I would like a shower now. And possibly somewhere to rest for a couple of hours.'

The key was hanging on a spare hook beside the cups.

He picked it up and went out, very obviously limping and in pain. They heard the front door open and close.

'I don't like him anymore,' she said.

'I have never liked him,' he reminded her. 'He's a liar. He lies when there is no point. Remember how he lied about Dimitar. Dimitar can't talk. When my father found him, way back in the seventies, he'd been taken hostage by a rival bandit gang in the mountains, and they'd cut out his tongue.'

She shivered.

Fool, he admonished himself. She didn't need to hear that. Or maybe she did. Maybe she needed reminding that they weren't playing games.

'I don't understand,' she said. 'Why can't we just stay here?'

'I believe he means that extra people can be close by, looking like ordinary people. So when something goes wrong, they can help.' He caught the hand that was intent on removing his empty plate. 'I don't think it is necessary for you to come anymore. He will drive. Surely you can remain here. Miss Arbanisi knows me, so there is no need at all for you to be present. If she is concerned about you, Frank will assure her that you are safe. Don't worry. He has no reason to bring you. From now on, you can . . .'

'How dare you?' She pulled her hand away.

'How dare I what?'

'Tell me not to worry. Where was that wise bit of advice last night?'

'I didn't . . .'

'No you didn't, did you? The only person you thought about was you! What would have happened to me, if you died? That didn't occur to you, did it?'

She was right. He had no answer. She waited and waited,

but he had no answer. Without warning she scooped his plate from the table and hurled it at the opposite wall. Then she ran from the room. He heard her feet pounding up the stairs.

He got up and went over to the wall, kneeling to gather the broken bits of china.

Chapter Forty-Two

'Oh,' Dina exclaimed, as they came in sight of the town.

'What?' Frank said.

He was driving, Feliks next to him. They both started, looking from side to side of the road.

'Nothing.'

It was a new house. She hadn't noticed it the night before. It would be quite grand when it was finished. Scaffolding stood round it, and the barrel of a concrete mixer, though unattended, was circling around. So many changes, in so few years. Well, why not? Just because a place was important to you, and you wanted to keep it safe, other people couldn't be stopped from changing it. If she cared that much she should be living here, getting involved, trying to preserve what mattered, like Irene trying to save her endangered sandcats. She could have finished her nursing course, or be doing B&B, or just living on less.

'Would there be landslides up there?' Frank asked. 'The hills are very severe.' He was right. But it wasn't so much their height as their bulk, and the unrelenting bare solidity of them. On both sides of the road, tufts of reeds grew in dense clumps, like bleached shaving brushes. Frank had let his window down a little. The smell of wood burning came in on the air as they approached the first row of houses.

He pulled out to give plenty of room to two women on large horses, one bay, one roan. Dina recognised one of riders. Annie Masson. She'd stayed on the island, going straight from school to work at the trekking centre. Annie had had her own pony, and two dogs. Mother had claimed to be allergic to animal hair. So, no dog, no cat, no rabbit in her childhood.

Feliks was watching her in the mirror.

'Nothing,' she said again, though no question had been asked.

He was angry because Frank had wanted her to come. Frank had washed and shaved and changed into clean clothes from a bag in the boot of his car. He'd rested upstairs in the room where Feliks had slept. She'd stayed in hers, apart from a long soak in the bathroom, so she had no idea what Feliks might or might not have done.

She didn't like Feliks so much anymore. Mostly because when he was around Frank he changed into someone else. The look on his face whenever Frank told them what they were to do was scary, the hostility in the air was so tangible you could have hung your coat on it. Right now Frank was driving rather slowly. He didn't believe Irene had got away from her kidnapper. We're taking no chances, he said. The police would be close at hand from now on, he said, but he didn't want any more surprises.

She didn't like Frank at all. Her stomach had gone tight when he'd turned on her, telling all the things she'd be arrested for. She'd been trying her best to be nice and all of a sudden there was real cruelty in his voice. She was back in Irene's narrow hallway, pressed against the wall, with a hand squeezing her waist, and a voice in her ear. Frank would never be cuddly again. She wouldn't be fooled. If there was any fooling to be done, Frank would be the one fooled.

They'd agreed to stop at the baker's shop in the main square where she and her school pals had often bought bacon rolls for lunch. On one side stood the Bank with its wrought iron railings, on the other the Dental Surgery. Of course Frank limped along beside her, leaning on Grampa MacLeod's walking stick. To pay, he said. But really it was to make sure she didn't fling herself on the floor or have a screaming fit or talk out of turn. As it turned out, she didn't even know any of the people serving or in the queue, which felt quite strange.

As they were walking back to the car, a voice hailed her from behind, 'Donaldina, is that you?'

Alan McNaught. Unchanged. The fair curly hair, the rosy cheeks, the big grin. Aged ten, she'd pulled back a chair he was about to sit on, in revenge for something, she couldn't recall what. She'd been sent to the headmistress, while her own father in his surgery inserted two stitches in Alan's wounded head. They'd been friends ever since. He was out of his police uniform, a sports bag slung over his shoulder.

She began in English, 'Alan, it's good to see you,' then changed to the Gaelic. 'Alan, keep smiling as I talk, can you?'

'Of course,' he smiled broadly. 'Is this fellow why we're not talking in English?' He gave Frank a nod.

'Yes, he is. I'm saying this as if Grampa MacLeod was beside me listening. So you understand I'm not joking. This man holding me by the arm is forcing me and my friend to do something. He says he's a policeman, but I don't think he is.'

'So, you are in some kind of bad trouble, and you want me to help. What do you want me to do? Does he have a weapon?'

'No. Laugh as if I've said something funny.'

Alan laughed loudly. 'Well, that's very good. However, I can perhaps detain him right now if you tell me a bit more. Would that be an idea?'

'Sorry to interrupt, but we should be going, Dina,' Frank warned her, 'These are getting cold.'

'Alan, can you keep us in sight, or get someone else to? I'm scared something very bad is going to happen. Around twelve o'clock.'

'Of course. Consider it done.'

Alan got hold of Frank's hand and shook it, then with a gesture midway between a salute and a wave turned away.

'Who was that? What was all that about?'

'Oh, I knew him at school,' she said. 'He's on his way to the swimming pool. He was asking if I was married yet, and I said he had never asked me.'

'You said quite a lot more than that.'

'Oh, not really. A little bit about who was still here and who had moved on. It takes a lot longer to say things in the Gaelic. Sometimes you have to turn whole sentences around.'

'He seems to have cheered you up. You look quite pleased with yourself.'

'Do I? Oh, that's terrible. Well, he told me I was looking very pretty, if you must know. Every girl likes a compliment.'

The car was parked down by the sea. The place was cluttered, just as she remembered, with buses, cars and boats in a state of disrepair, smells of fried food and diesel and seaweed. There was a strong wind blowing inshore. She got into the back of the car again. Frank stood outside to eat his bacon rolls but his window was open. So there was no chance to share her cleverness.

'Why are you smiling?' Feliks asked.

'Am I?'

'She met her old boyfriend,' Frank said loudly. 'I think love is in the air.'

Chapter Forty-Three

Dina led the way along an earth path, trodden to brick hardness between thin ridges of tree roots that had always reminded her of the dried-out sinews of dead sheep. When they emerged onto the field, the wind from the sea brought the taste of salt to her mouth. Crows were taking off against the wind, landing clumsily in the tall pines around the circle of rough grass. What was the point of crows? Their cawing was one of the ugliest sounds in all creation.

She pulled the sleeves of her sweater down over her hands. The past was all around her. Year after year they'd gathered here to watch the Games. Crowds of islanders and tourists. The drone of the pipes tuning up, the smell of sausages from the food vans, the cheese stall with samples on paper plates, and cubes of bread to dip in flavoured oils. And there she was herself, part of the junior school choir, facing disaster. Chrisanne their angel-voiced soloist was late. Mrs Taylor, immense and buoyant in her white shoes and white-collared navy dress, moved from foot to foot in anxiety . . .

The old Scots pine trees bent to the left away from the prevailing wind as they had always done. One had broken in a previous winter's gale, its trunk now safely levelled off near the ground. The rest stood proud and high, bushy only at the very top. Grey gulls floated overhead. Some pecked about with the crows and sparrows for anything worth eating in the grass.

Her earlier cheerful feeling of bravado had evaporated. What if she was wrong, and Frank was exactly what he said he was? She'd be in massive trouble. She'd be in for the biggest humiliation of her life. Her insides felt tight, exactly the way they did when waiting for the dentist, knowing that you'd not been nearly scrupulous enough, but hoping she wouldn't notice, when the reality was that she always noticed.

Frank told them to sit on one of the benches. He sat on one a little way off, with a magazine, wearing sunglasses though the sun wasn't shining. Two teenage boys were cycling round the grass. One tossed a can towards a big stone litter bin. It bounced off the rim. He stopped, went backwards, legs wide, picked it up and tried again, successfully. They cycled back into the trees.

'I always had to wear a helmet.'

'What?' Feliks said.

'On a bike. I had to wear my helmet.'

If only there was a helmet that could keep out of her head the memories that were beginning to close in on every side. The old house, just the chimneys visible from here. Would the swing still be there? The greenhouse? She hadn't gone back since the new people moved in. It was almost six years now. Three since Grampa's death. Mrs Thomson who'd cleaned for them after Mother left was still alive. There was still a card at Christmas.

It was after twelve. Away to their left, there was a sign lying on its side. *Danger. No Access Beyond This Point.* She closed her eyes. The wind was rushing through the tree tops. She heard traffic sounds, the rattle of a boat engine starting up, a dog barking far away.

'I won a gold medal here once, at the Games. Well, the choir did. Chrisanne was so good. It's strange how you lose things that sometimes you thought you would die before you lost them.'

She'd kept it in a pink musical box. You had to keep the boxes locked. Keep it all locked, all the sorrow, but the joy too, because that was the price one had to pay. All the good memories, the days that . . .

'So, you can sing.'

'Actually, yes. I'm quite good. Are you?'

'I don't know.'

'How can you not know? What are you good at?'

'I told you before. Throwing stones.'

'D'you think Irene's coming?' she said.

No answer.

'Can I ask you something else? I was wondering, if she went back with you, would she be safe?'

She thought he wasn't going to answer this question either but he did.

'I don't know. I think she will be all right.'

She hoped so, she really did, because she thought Irene would want to go. Irene loved being special, being the centre of attention and having nice things like the emerald ring. And who was she to be judging Irene? She was just as greedy for nice things. She'd been furious, angry and jealous when the old house was sold without a word of warning, and everything shipped to Spain. Mother had sold her small flat and bought a villa to house them in. She herself had glibly told everyone she wanted only memories, but really she'd been seething inside for ages. Grampa's quiet words, 'the croft will be all yours, Donaldina' hadn't helped, because she didn't want him to die too.

Beside her, Feliks stiffened. She saw why. Irene in front, the blond man behind her. They were walking down the curved road that led to the park. They'd be hidden behind the first trees in a minute. She'd lied. Why had she lied to them? She hadn't lost him at all. Unless she had and he'd found her again.

'Promise me one thing,' Feliks said. 'No matter what happens, no matter what anyone says to you, even me, keep behind me.' He was kicking at the stones around the concrete base under the bench.

'Behind you?'

'I mean, let no one reach you, get hold of you. No one, not even Miss Arbanisi. Keep your eye on Frank especially. Stay behind me and out of everyone's way. Don't try to help. Promise me.' His hands were her shoulders, then lightly on the sides of her face, holding her so she couldn't look away.

She couldn't promise. If she did, she wouldn't be free to do something if there was something that needed doing. It would be like opening the biggest box in the universe. Anything might happen.

'Promise me.'

'All right,' she said.

Chapter Forty-Four

Feliks let her go. Could he do this thing? As easily make a perfect bottle out of the fractured glass lying there beside the refuse bin. And what of his own future? If he succeeded now, there would be no going back. *I want your wings*, he told the white birds wheeling overhead. *Take me with you. Take me to the land where bananas grow.*

He saw Frank fold his magazine and take out his mobile phone. De Bono and the woman were still out of sight but it wouldn't be long. He rehearsed once more how the thing might be done. Someone emerged out of the trees, but it was merely a workman, young but wearing a flat cap like an old man's. He was clad in overalls, pushing a blue bin on wheels, with a spiked metal pole attached to it. A bunch of black plastic bags hung on the bin handle. The young man walked across the grass to the concrete litter bin, and began pushing about in it with the pole. A small black dog came dancing across to him from the opposite direction, snuffling at his ankles, only to be called sharply back by its owner, a burly man in a red anorak.

Charles arrived first. He paused momentarily at the end of the path where it met the short grass, then began to come forward. Irene was a few paces behind. She seemed to be struggling with the tree roots, uncertain whether to step over or avoid them. Feliks glanced at the birds in the wind, and waited and waited. Charles half turned to see whether she was following, then turned to walk on, and at precisely the right moment Feliks let the stone fly. Charles crumpled, fell on his back, his arms high.

For a couple of seconds nothing happened, then shouts and screams merged. He turned his back on them all, kneeling down on the concrete to face Dina, pulling her to him. She wasn't screaming or yelling, for which he was thankful. She was rigid for a while, then she relaxed. Her head rested on his neck. He could feel her breath on his skin.

'I'm not going to leave you,' he said, not sure if she heard him.

But there were hands on his upper arms, pulling him away. More than one person's hands. And everyone was shouting. At him, or at one another? He gave up. His head was held, forced down, and his body with it, and now someone heavy was sitting on his back. His arms were yanked round, his wrists cuffed. So be it, he thought. So be it.

Chapter Forty-Five

'Alone at last. We should be breaking out the champagne,' Frank said, easing himself into the other armchair, hooking his borrowed walking stick over the arm. 'This isn't quite the same, but you're welcome to have one.'

He offered a whisky miniature. Berisovic shook his head.

Frank didn't bother with a glass. He wasn't really a whisky drinker, but he was weary to his bones. Berisovic had surprised him completely, but on reflection it had been done well. He was rubbing his wrists, but there hadn't been a word of complaint, which was very sensible of him, all things considered. The MacLeod girl was sleeping upstairs, and Irene Arbanisi, having talked at length to Berisovic and himself, was resting under sedation in the Cottage Hospital. Charles de Bono was, he glanced at his watch, by now undergoing emergency surgery, having been flown to the mainland. From which surgery he would most probably recover. It didn't much matter. The forces of law and order would wend their dutiful way onwards. De Bono was no longer his problem.

'You don't look happy.'

Berisovic came back from whatever distant place he'd been in. 'Why should I be happy? My companion has died, and I have almost killed someone. To say nothing of that.' He gestured to Frank's leg.

'You did what you came to do. You spoke to the Countess. Your mission is a success.'

'I suppose. Yes.'

'You don't feel it was worthwhile?'

'What I feel doesn't matter.'

Frank doubted this. Berisovic was a man of strong feelings. He almost envied him. It was so long since he had known what his own were. The sudden thought disturbed him. He tried to picture his children, and their mother, as he always did when things threatened to fall apart, but when they took shape they were looking at one another, not at him.

'Tell me, why did you agree to come in the first place?' he asked.

'My father promised to release some friends of mine. I don't know if he will or not.'

And that was all?

'What happens now?' Berisovic asked.

Frank took another sip. The question had been a long time coming. He felt almost sorry it had to come at all.

'You don't have to worry about her,' he pointed to the ceiling. 'Well, not as far as I'm concerned. Contrary to what I said earlier, there won't be any charges against her. She's not going to bounce back in a day or two, but she'll be all right. She's stronger than she thinks. I suspect when you grow up with that kind of stuff, some of it sticks.'

'What stuff?'

'I asked her what it said.' He pointed to the calligraphy on the wall. "The sin it will us down to waters deep, the grace it will us safely back to land." Apparently they don't do verbs in Gaelic.'

Berisovic leaned back in his chair.

A useful language, verbs or no verbs, Frank thought, when you wanted to deceive. A cunning little lady. She'd fooled him completely. If he'd not been a bit off his game, with all the medication and so forth, he'd have caught on. He'd have recognised the young man with the rubbish bin as the friend she'd chatted to earlier. He might even have suspected that the dog knew the fellow, and that its owner in the red jacket was not a mere bystander, though he couldn't have guessed they were the local law enforcement, constable and sergeant.

Well, it had required more than grace to get them all out of deep waters this time. It had taken many hours, and several phone calls to undo her cleverness, to persuade the local law that he had a special interest in these people, that no one wanted arresting but De Bono, that co-operation rather than help was needed, that all was well in the best of all possible worlds. Which it soon would be. Even the motorbike would be safely back in its own garage before too long.

'What will you do with me?'

It was said so quietly, Frank almost missed it. He'd half a mind not to answer.

'If it was up to me . . .'

'I think it is up to you,' Berisovic said. 'I think it has always been up to you.'

Frank rubbed the horn handle on the walking stick. It was nicely carved, a long Celtic knot weaving in and out of itself. The symbol for eternity, he recalled. They'd been great ones for eternity, those ancient Celts. Eternity and bogs and bloodshed. Not unlike himself.

Berisovic wasn't done. 'Of course, I mean it in a philosophical sense. I believe you have always made decisions that suited you. Perhaps even from boyhood. And all the time people have admired you. You see, I know how it feels. One must go on, success after success, because failure is out of the question. This is of course the behaviour of an idiot, to continue when there is nothing of value to be gained and when, if one does not succeed, there is only a black hole waiting, larger than anything we can imagine.'

'What do you want me to say?'

'Am I making decisions now?'

'No, you're not. Neither am I. To be perfectly honest, there's more than one set of strings being pulled here. The first option was that Miss Arbanisi would die and you would take the blame.'

'Whose decision was that?'

'I think it was your father's, though I wasn't told. It never seemed to me like the ideal option for a man in his position. But you know him better than I do. My own feeling is that it was based more on spite than common sense. And then, when it didn't look like that was going to work out, other options came into play. The Countess will decide to accept your offer or she won't. Then it depends on . . .'

'Will she be safe?'

'How would I know? Not my problem. As I was about to say, I imagine her future will depend on who is willing to pay the best price for the oil.'

'So who precisely are you working for? The British? The Americans?'

It was curious that Berisovic didn't mention his father. Or the Russians.

'Look at it this way. In the real world, it's always about money and power. Always has been, always will be. God, I'm talking in clichés again. I hate that.'

'And me?'

'Oh, you die anyway.'

'I don't go to prison? Not even for my stone throwing?'

'Too risky.'

'I can't simply retire?' Berisovic was speaking to the wall.

'You may as well die. Nobody wants you.'

Was this true? Frank thought of the girl upstairs. He

supposed she might want him, in spite of everything. She probably liked the 'scarred hero' idea. Her head was full of romantic nonsense.

Berisovic lifted his head. 'That may be so, yet I think I prefer to live. I think I am ready to live. And I must ask you, does anyone want you, Frank? You were born to be a human being, but you are a tool. Don't you see? A tool is all you are. Was that what you were meant to be in this life?'

'I told you, this isn't personal.'

Without even telling Berisovic to remain where he was, he went out to the car. The gun was lost to him, but he would never have used the gun anyway. The small brown leather case was in the boot, next to his sports bag. He unlocked it and checked the contents. He reminded himself once more that this wasn't personal, that it was nothing new, that it was simply a job, but all he could really think of was how he'd played badminton brilliantly for years, only realising when he finally stopped how long and how deeply he'd hated it. He looked back at the house. He stared at the little brown box for some time, then re-locked it.

He closed the boot. Getting into the driver's seat, he put the walking stick on the passenger side and fastened his safety belt. He started the engine and, out of habit, checked the mirrors. He eased himself out onto the empty road. One of his employers would be momentarily baffled, would ask some awkward questions, would hum and haw, then accept his report and reassign him. The others he decided, could go to hell.

Postscript

Janek had not been sleeping well for some time. His life had become difficult and quite stressful after the disappearance of Lazslo Christescu and, having taken a tablet after an ample supper, he did not on this autumn evening hear the loud knocking at his door. His housekeeper however was still up and dressed. She answered the knocking, a little surprised to find two men in coats, as the air outside was still warm. She liked the house. Hot weather made her ankles swell, but the house had been pleasantly cool all summer, thanks to the air conditioning that had been recently installed.

She didn't know these men who had come to speak to her boss and hold him responsible for crimes against the state, including conspiracy to murder. She knew nothing of what he had done or not done. He was not a nice man, that she knew, but she had never troubled herself with anything except cleaning and cooking. Cleaning was her passion. She noted with satisfaction that the two strangers wiped their shoes on the mat, and addressed her politely. She didn't ask questions. She had never asked questions, which was why she had kept her job for a long time. She knew she was not a very clever woman. But on the other hand she wasn't stupid either, and as she watched them proceed upstairs, she sensed that despite all the advantages of working for a tidy, single government official for a good salary in an air-conditioned house, it might be time to look for a new employer.

On another night, in a different part of the city, an elderly man with an Asiatic cast to his features genuflected briefly as he entered a small building. It was not an important building, being tucked into a side street in an unfashionable corner of the city, and hardly anyone ever attended. It was dark inside. Only a few candles gave light at the front. He slipped onto a bench near the back, and began to recite, by the movement of his hands, a short prayer. It was generally the same prayer. He asked forgiveness for his sins, especially for the sin of continued faithfulness to a man whom he knew to be wicked. On this particular night however, he added to his regular confession a small thank you. There was a crumpled piece of paper inside his waistcoat. It had travelled by a long and roundabout way to reach him. It read, '*The plum tree has been transplanted, and seems to be well suited to its new soil.*'